Chasing Butterflies

RICHIE SINGH

ISBN: 0615544258
ISBN-13: 978-0615544250 (GNO and A)

TO LIFE

CONTENTS

RICHIE SINGH

CHASING BUTTERFLIES

ACKNOWLEDGMENTS

God. Family. Friends. And Others

NECESSARY MUMBO JUMBO

PART 1

1 Beginnings

"There are two mistakes one can make along the road to truth...not going all the way, and not starting."
(Hindu Prince Gautama Siddhartha, the founder of Buddhism)

There are three fundamental goals that every Indian parent dreams of crossing off their life list before their kids hit 27.

1. Stable, well-paying job, preferably with a respectable big company.
2. Sweet homely *bahu* (daughter-in law) or smart successful son in law.
3. Adorable grand baby to show off to Mrs. Sharma (or whoever your nosy neighbor may be).

If said goals are not achieved by age 27, like most loving and accommodating parents, they compromise and develop a new set of muted goals to be achieved before the magical age of 30. However, they then set out to accomplish this new 3-point agenda with a sense of divine fanaticism that would put even the Taliban to shame.

1. Any job or form of gainful employment.
2. A *bahu* who does not shout back or a reasonably non-creepy son in law.
3. Faint glimmer of seeing grandkids before the great *tirath* (pilgrimage).

Unfortunately, with Bear Stearns collapsing and the world economy in shambles, goal #1 seemed on very shaky ground. Add to that the lack of a steady girlfriend in the near past, goal #2 seemed unrealistic as well. And I think the parents were quite sure that they'd rather not see any grandkids until goal #2 was achieved.

But with a paycheck still trickling in, and a son closer to 27 than to 30, there was still the *audacity to hope* that things could be corrected. In a magnanimous gesture, I was given the grand option of either finding a bride on matrimonial websites myself, or being actively shopped around by the parents.

Now what do you think would a rational (and admittedly, somewhat ready to settle down) 28 year old choose?

By the way, I must apologize for not introducing myself earlier. The boy in question is myself, Toby Arora. Before you ask, no one really knows why I was named Toby. One family legend is that while fighting in the Second World War, my grandfather's life was saved by a soldier named Toby. Overcome by gratitude, he swore an oath that he would name his first grandchild after him. That first grandchild happened to be me. Another legend is that my mother heard the name Toby in a dream and took it as a sign from God. My father tried telling her that what she heard when she was half asleep was the *'dhobi'* (laundry guy) announcing that he was at the door. But once he realized his argument wasn't making any headway with my mother, he decided to believe that it was a God given name as well.

All this happened 28 years ago. Now, 28 years later, they felt that they had another divine calling. This time, it was to set their son on the path of marriagehood, and then parenthood, before the big three-o. As a consequence, here I was, trying to dip my fingers into the world of online Indian matchmaking.

Creating a profile on matrimony.com was a very conflicted exercise. 'What part of my personality did I want to highlight in my profile? Did I want to come across as someone generic or someone different? What perfect words and adjectives described me? Are there perfect words? Did I even know myself well enough?'

Eventually, I decided I was special (aren't we all?) and my profile had to be unique and out of the ordinary. Highlighting my humorous side (as well as lazy), I flirted with the idea of porting my semi-inspired match.com profile.

I am a normal laid back individual looking for someone equally normal and laid back. I get along well with most people, and most people get along well with me.

I have a simple life. I wake up in the morning, and after a few battles with the alarm clock, manage to drag myself out of bed. After coffee or tea (or both), I head to work. In the evening, I come back from work. Occasionally I go to the gym, but mostly I end up hanging out with a few buds. Then I sleep, and the cycle repeats.

Weekends are slightly different. I almost always win my battle with the alarm clock, and for the most part, avoid work like the plague and indulge in more meaningful and fun activities like doing nothing.

The idea was immediately shot down by my younger sister who minced no words in her email response.

Are you nuts? This is cheesy and immature. *Tu maa baap ki izzat mitti me milayega* (you will bring shame to the whole family).

She then responded with a version that was probably drafted and redrafted at least five times by the parents. It was to the point and promptly addressed what is considered the most important criteria in a prospective groom.

Hint: It's not about the kind of person I am.

Our son has an MBA and Bachelors in Sociology from leading US universities with an excellent academic record. He is currently working as a manager in USA in a prestigious Fortune 500 company.

Then some additional marketing:

We belong to a respectable Sikh family of highly educated professionals settled in India. Our other child, a daughter, has just finished her master's from a leading Indian university also with an excellent academic record. We believe that marriage is not only a faithful, loving, caring and respectful bond, but also a life-long positive relationship between two families.

Then #2 on the list:

We are looking for an educated and homely girl that we can treat as our daughter.

And finally #3 on the list, with a veiled reference to the son frequenting bars and lounges and imbibing alcohol (gasp!)

Our son is friendly, outgoing, has an active lifestyle and is looking forward to settling down to a life of marital bliss and contentment.

Alarmed, I promptly sent an email to my sister

Did you guys find a long-lost sibling who was lost at some *'mela'* many years ago and just returned home? Looks like you wrote up a profile for someone else. This sounds 'cheesier'.

Her reply was quick, as if anticipating my reaction

Well no. Actually you don't know it, but you are adopted. Someone left you at our doorstep in a basket. You never wondered why your name is Toby and not some typical Punjabi name that ends in 'inder' or 'preet'? It was because the basket had a name tag attached to it which said Toby. This is how they expected their kid to be before *tu bigar gaya. Kya karein, apna khoon apna aur paraya khoon toh paraya hota hai* (Literal translation: You are spoilt! Alas, what can we do! Your bloodline is your own, and someone else's someone else's).

Not to be dissuaded, I spent some extra thought on my next move. Clearly, the above was unacceptable. One, it did not distinguish me from the thousands of eligible bachelors out there. Two, it sounded like it had been copied from some cheap paperback (ironic, yes) with the sole purpose of impressing through a flowery application of the Queen's language.

Now, I, Toby Arora, refuse to be generic. And as for flowery language, I can do better. So out came the dusty old notebooks dotted with poetry written during the lazy days of college. After all, everything is fair in love and war, and this profile creation exercise was turning into a small skirmish.

Sometimes I have this dream,
a dream that leaves me with wonder.
Wonder if I can reach out towards its innocence,
to touch it and to feel it,
and hold it like a butterfly in my hand.

Sometimes I have this dream,
a dream that leaves me feeling free.
Free to play in the limitless sky,
to jump from one cloud to another,
and each cloud with its own special joy.

Sometimes I have this dream,
a dream that leaves me with peace.
Peace as if the world stops and leaves me with a moment,
to gift me everything I need in that moment,
and that one pure moment lasts forever.

Sometimes I have this dream,
a dream that leaves me with hope.
Hope that someday I'll chase down my rainbow,
to find at its end, you,
and with you spend that one pure moment.

The response to this was much more muted and direct.

Ok fine, you may not be adopted. But if you don't get serious about this
thing, your parents are prepared to disown you.
And your poetry sucks.

It wasn't that I was not serious. Granted, I was skeptical about the
idea of a matrimony website. But more importantly, as you inch
closer to the magical age of 30, you do notice the pool of eligible
candidates getting slimmer. You also tend to get a bit more set in
your ways, and perhaps a bit more cynical about the world in general
and love in particular. All this does make it harder to find someone
who is the right fit. I was more than cognizant of this fact.

But, growing up, I had realized one important secret about the art of
parent management. More often than not, they are never too happy
with the first one or two ideas you come up with, especially if they
don't fit their version of the world. I quickly learnt to use this golden
nugget to my advantage by always starting off by surprising them
with one or two extreme ideas. The *shock and awe* that this created

then allowed us to compromise on a solution that was much more reasonable and left everyone happy. The parents were happy because they were able to influence me from my irrational position. I was happy because I ended up with something closer to what I originally wanted. This was so much better than communicating what I wanted and then starting a long and messy bargaining exercise. If John Nash hadn't beaten me to it, the win-win solution would be associated not with the prisoner's dilemma but the parent-kid dilemma. (There are a lot of books on parenting out there. I am convinced, however, that if someone wrote a book on managing parents for kids, it would outsell Harry Potter).

After protracted negotiations, threats and blackmail, we eventually settled on a reasonable and simple (and slightly clichéd) representation of Toby that kept everyone happy.

I'd describe myself as liberal, optimistic and somewhat idealistic with a blend of eastern and western values. I grew up in Chandigarh and moved to the US for undergrad and graduate school. I currently work as a manager in a consulting company. I am ambitious but also like to keep a work life balance.

I like exploring and learning about new things, from the eclectic to the mundane, am fascinated by ancient history as well as science fiction, and have recently developed a fondness for travel.

I am probably looking for someone similar (or maybe completely opposite). Chemistry is the key.

So that's how this story started. With the creation of the perfect "I" profile.

Well almost. There was still one important ingredient missing. A justification or rationale for why I was on the website and a slightly more stellar opening. My research indicated the following were the top 3 rationales used across profiles:

1. I created a profile because work does not leave enough free time to go out and meet new people
2. I heard good things about the website from friends/family and decided to try it out
3. It's hard to write about yourself on a website. But I created this profile to help me find a good life partner.

I chose number 2.

And so began the journey down this road.

2 Winner Winner Chicken Dinner

The man who said I'd rather be lucky than good saw deeply into life.
(From the movie Match Point)

Toby's Journal
Entry 13, 2009

We believe we deserve a lot of things.

A legendary love story.
A storybook castle.
A frog that turns into a prince.
Or a beautiful princess on a high tower.

There is perfection. Somewhere.

Pyramus had Thesbe, who found each other by nightly whispers through a crack in a shared wall.

Shirn had Khusrow, who journeyed many a miles, many a times, until they found each other.

Tristan had Isolde, who were bound by fate and a magical love potion.

Point is, there is perfection. Somewhere.

All you have to do is to find it.

-X-

With thousands of profiles available at the click of a button, I was quite confident that I had a better shot at finding someone perfect than anyone else before me. Until I actually started looking.

I soon came to realize that it wasn't that easy. You see, finding the perfect partner is a lot like playing roulette (affinity towards gambling was also something my parents thought was adequately explained by the word 'active lifestyle').You summon your highest facilities of logic and analyses (not that it matters much), combine it with the intuition in your gut that everything feels right, and put all your money on a single number. The dealer spins the wheel in one direction and then drops a ball in the other direction. In time, the ball starts to slow down, and starts bouncing between slots of different numbers, as you watch with your fingers crossed. Eventually, it stops at a number. The one you picked!?

My initial approach was quite similar, partly out of laziness, and partly out of being extremely busy at work. Every day, the website emailed me a dozen profiles that it thought were perfect for me. Every night, I looked through those profiles to see if anyone piqued my interest. This continued for a few weeks with limited success until my parent's spokeswoman cornered me online on Google talk.

Ru: Hi bro
Me: Hey! Sup?

Ru: Can't sleep. So did you find anyone yet?
Me: No
Ru: Hmm.. Did you talk to anyone yet?
Me: No
Ru: Did you at least TRY to talk to anyone yet?
Me: No
Ru: Why?
Me: They send me this email with matches. Just a dozen or so, not that many. So it takes time
Ru: They have a search function you know. Make some effort
Me: It's a bit busy at work too
Ru: Do you want us to search and shortlist for you?

Although time was an extremely limited resource, the last thing I wanted to do was to hand over access to my account to my sister and parents. I was pretty confident that there activities wouldn't be limited to just searching for and short listing profiles. Them initiating interest was a certain possibility and my sister sending a 'hello' email on my behalf to speed things along was a possibility that could not be ruled out either.

I quickly backtracked and tried to do some damage control.

Me: It's not really the volume. I just haven't seen any profiles that clicked
Ru: If you search, you will see more profiles and find someone you might like
Ru: I am free for the next few weeks. I can search for you and shortlist profiles. That's the least I can do for my dear brother

I had to concede that she did make sense and promised to look into the search function. I was also getting more comfortable with the idea of a matrimonial website and was quite curious to discover what else was out there. So, I decided to allocate a little bit of time in the evenings and become a bit more deliberate in my quest for perfection.

For someone used to the simplicity of Google, the search function was a bit overwhelming. I did not expect that I could type the keyword 'perfect partner for me' and be able to find the right profile within the first three pages of results. However, neither did I expect to be confronted with over a 100 different options for attributes I would like in a potential partner. To be honest, I did not have much of checklist or must-have attributes. What I was searching for was an abstract commodity called chemistry which wasn't really limited to age, height, occupation etc. Unfortunately, chemistry wasn't one of the myriad of options presented by the search engine. Age, height and occupation were. So I did the next best thing and started working backwards from the absolute must-not-have's. That helped a little bit and for a few weeks I was happily browsing an array of very diverse profiles. A few weeks later, I had another conversation with my sister which had a sense of déjà vu.

Ru: Hi bro
Me: Hey! Sup?
Ru: So did you figure out the search function yet?
Me: It's not that bad
Ru: Good. Find anyone yet?
Me: No
Ru: Did you talk to anyone yet?
Me: No
(I could sense a gasp)
Ru: Did you at least TRY to talk to anyone yet?
Me: No

Before she could ask the proverbial 'why', I typed in what I thought would be an acceptable explanation.

Me: It takes time to find someone you click with

Unfortunately, there is nothing like an acceptable explanation when your whole family is committed to just one goal.

Ru: *Tujhe sharam nahin aati. Tere ghar mein ek budhi aandhi maa hai jo har roz darwaze pe beth kar aapne beta ka intezaar karti hai, ek budha baap hai jisne saari zindagi factory mein mazdoori kar ke tujhe school bheja, ek behan hai jo budhi ho rahi hai aur uski shaadi nahin ho rahi kyonki log dahej ke liye ek lakh mangte hain*
Me: Mom's not blind, Dad's never been close to a factory, and you haven't even turned 21

Ru: That's just fine print. I was watching an old Hindi movie. I think I should become a heroine in some saas bahu show.

Me: Yep. Try for the mother-in-law role

Ru: Shut up. So, if you don't even talk to anyone, how would you find out if you have chemistry with someone?

And after a brief pause

Ru: Mama is asking 'Are you even serious about this?' Should we give an ad in the newspaper?

Again, she did have a good point and an equally good threat. Though not perfect, there were a few profiles that had made me curious and piqued my interest. Maybe this website business was a good idea. Well, at least better than a newspaper. Work was easing off a little as well which allowed me the time to actually pursue some of the profiles I'd shortlisted. So, once again, I decided to be a bit more deliberate and proactive and plunge head-on into the 4 step process of finding true love (the Indian online matrimonial way).

Step 1 was to search and shortlist. This was easily achieved.

Step 2 was to express interest and be 'accepted'. This was a bit harder than I had anticipated.

Apparently, there was a reason behind the myriad of options or attributes in potential partners. Not everyone was as open-ended as me. Most women had certain criteria that were must-haves, which eliminated a good number of profiles that I had considered interesting. I expected people to have constraints around religion, age etc., the usual suspects. But had my parents warned me that not being an engineer or a doctor would be a handicap when it came time to get married, I would have reconsidered selecting sociology as an undergraduate major. For a brief period during my bachelors, I had considered choosing English literature as my major. I don't even wish

13

to imagine what that would have done to my matrimonial attractiveness!

The first few interests that I expressed were declined because I wasn't an engineer. I have to admit I am fairly thick skinned. Rejection did not dissuade me much. That and it was a bit too late to go back and get an engineering degree. Luckily, the website had foreseen exactly such a scenario and developed a handy tool that allowed me to filter results to profiles whose requirements I met. That shrunk the universe a little bit (well quite a bit, to be honest), but gave me a universe where initial rejection would not be based on occupation but more on the way I looked and the ramblings in my profile. An acceptable compromise!

In time, I had a healthy number of interesting profiles lined up. A small group of prospects who I was excited to know more about and who had been interested enough to accept me and allow me the opportunity to initiate contact with them.

Step 3 in the great Indian online matrimonial search was to initiate contact. The first communication.

The website provided three methods for first contact. One was to send a message through an internal email system. Second was to chat in real time using a custom messenger. Third was the good old option to share a telephone number. There should have been a fourth option. Telepathy.

Walt Whitman famously said in one of his poems:

> *"Stranger. If you passing meet me, and desire to speak to me, why should you not speak to me?*
> *And why should I not speak to you?"*

Clearly, he hadn't run into Indian matrimonial websites.

A week after the last conversation, my sister cornered me for a status update.

Ru: Hi. How's the search going?
Me: Ok
Ru: Ok?
Me: Yes
Ru: Why?
Me: Well. It's kind of hard to get in touch with people
Ru: How so?
Me: So finally a few women I was interested in accepted my interest. Naturally I sent them a message to say hello. And then nothing really happened
Ru: What kind of message are you sending?
Me: Basic. Hi this is Toby. Liked your profile and would love to know more. We can communicate via email at tobyarora31@gmail.com or at 3121313131
Ru: and..
Me: A couple replied back. One replied back with a one word message, 'Hi'. Then there were a few who didn't reply back which didn't make sense. And one declined me after I sent a hello message as if I committed some grave crime
Ru: Haha! Maybe they didn't like your name. Wait for a minute. Brb
Me: Sure
Ru: Back. So I googled your name. Nothing untoward showed up
Me: Very funny! You all would know if I'd done something 'untoward'
Ru: Still. That's how it is here. You've been in the US too long. Just talk to those who you are able to talk too. Ignore the rest
Me: Not very polite. But there are still a few interesting ones left
Ru: Cool! Your mom is saying she's glad that you are getting serious about this. It's high time you settled down

Step 4 in the great Indian online matrimonial search was to try to get a connection; to actually talk to someone and try to get to know them.

Now talking isn't that hard. We humans tend to do it all the time. Having a meaningful conversation though is slightly harder. But having a meaningful conversation under the pressure of a prospective matrimonial alliance and with the knowledge that everything you say is going to be analyzed and judged is a significantly greater challenge.

You try to limit the awkwardness by starting off with small talk. This is relatively simple.

Me: Hey, how's it going?
Her: Hey. Good. How are you?
Me: Good. Thanks for accepting my interest. I really liked your profile
Hey: No problem. I liked your profile as well

After some customary conversation about the weather, it's time to move on to a different topic. More often than not, it was work and education. Then family. Then if you're lucky something in common followed by the invariable 'what are your expectations from a partner?'

The first few conversations were unexpected. Instead of a regular conversation, let alone a conversation where you can be yourself and enjoy getting to know someone, it seemed more like a back and forth question answer session. One person even sent me a 5 page word document with really probing questions that she expected me to fill up in about a thousand words (or more) and send it back to her. And oh, it came with a countdown. If I took more than an hour to fill it out, it wouldn't be spontaneous enough.

For me, finding love could not be so mechanical and impersonal. I decided to try to steer the conversation more towards getting to know the other person instead of indulging in a two way interrogation session. Humor, I was convinced, would be a good way to break the formality and would result in a much friendlier conversation.

And the first guinea pig was Nisha.

Nisha: So what are your expectations from a partner?
Me: Well, someone who's laid back, takes it easy. It'll be good to have a few things in common. Obviously, attraction has to be there too
Nisha: That's not much
Me: Really, I think it boils down to chemistry. You never know who you'll find the right chemistry with
Nisha: Cool

There are moments in life when a voice in your head tells you 'Hey, this is a perfect moment to showcase your superb sense of humor and make a funny comment.' Then as soon as you act on it, another voice magically appears in your head. "Oops!"

Me: Well there's more. She has to be able to cook. I expect a lavish spread at dinner. When I come back tired from work, she should take my shoes off and massage my head. Then once in a while, when I get drunk, she should be fine with me yelling at her for no reason.

Nisha logged out. I guess some people don't get sarcasm. We connected again. I apologized and told her I was joking. She accepted my apology and I kept my humor in check. Eventually, it fizzled out. Our differences weren't limited to our sense of humor. Once momentum is lost, it's hard to regain it.

There was also a very important lesson from this incident. My sense of humor didn't come across that well over the Internet. Perhaps the beginning of getting to know someone was not the best time for sarcasm.

Unfortunately, I did not learn that lesson.

Wit and sarcasm were an inherent part of my personality. It was something a prospective partner would be exposed to on an ongoing basis, and I didn't see much logic in trying to hide it and pretend to be someone I wasn't. I convinced myself that it wasn't the humor that was the problem, it was just that it was a poor choice of humor.

Soon I connected with someone interesting; someone who not only appreciated my sense of humor, but also matched it. Email quickly graduated to phone and chat.

Rhea: So have you ever been to Michigan?
Me: Nope. Is it any good?

17

Rhea: Yes. You should come check it out sometime
Me: Ok. I'll start walking
Rhea: Lol. Ok. I'll see you in a few days
Me: If I make it. It's a long walk
Rhea: If you don't think you can, I will pick you up on the way so you are not standing in some unknown city with cows and chickens
Me: Is that what I'll get to see in Michigan?
Rhea: Along the way. Then you get to the city
Me: Are there any wheat fields in Michigan?
Rhea: No. But you should see corn fields
Me: That will work. Maybe I'll click a picture with the cows and chicken, and send a postcard to my parents. 'Hello from Michigan! Looks just like home.'
Rhea: Lol. They will be so proud
Me: So, jokes apart, the city..
Rhea: Yes
Me: It doesn't have any cows and chicken?
Rhea: No
Me: I'm disappointed
Rhea: Why?
Me: No fresh lassi and tandoori chicken
Rhea: Lol. Is that what you were thinking of when I said cows and chickens?
Me: Chicken is the state bird of Punjab
Rhea: You mean Tandoori Chicken
Me: Yummy!
Rhea: We have ducks in our backyard
Me: I've never had tandoori duck
Rhea: My ducks?
Me: Oops. That's insensitive. You've probably named the ducks
Rhea: Lol. They don't have names. They just come to the water fountain and we give them food
Me: Thank god
Rhea: Why?
Me: It'd be pretty hard to eat food if it had names. Imagine a chef saying, 'Today, our special is a tandoori duck called Donald, and broccoli called Sharmili."
Rhea: Lol. Doubt anyone would want broccoli and tandoori duck, no matter what it's named
Me: I shouldn't ever try to be a chef, I guess
Rhea: For the sake of humanity, never

In roulette, the highest odds are for a straight up. You put your money on a number. If the ball stops at that number, you get a 35 to 1 payout. When someone new to the game achieves a straight up, it's called beginners luck. Rhea and I were getting along pretty well. Maybe Rhea was a straight up. Maybe I had beginner's luck.

In time, we ended up on one of the more awkward topics that crops up when you are trying to know someone: the topic of religious beliefs. Now, for a 28 year old in a world overflowing with distractions, religion wasn't a topic I had delved on much. And the day it came up, I was in a particularly creative mood.

Rhea: So are you religious?
Me: Not really. I have friends from all kinds of faiths, and as long as you incentivize me with food, I will show up at any random religious festival
Rhea: No belief in organized religion
Me: More spiritual than traditional
Rhea: Why?
Me: Just don't think I fit into any specific religion
Rhea: Haha. Come up with your own religion
Me: That's not a bad idea. You can become one of my prophets.
Rhea: Well, you will need a book to spread your teachings. Do you have any?
Me: No. Could you possibly come up with a few and show me a first draft by Sunday?
Rhea: Lol. Sure. EBook ok?
Me: Perfect. Maybe we can get Amazon to be a sponsor and give out 'The holy Kindle'
Rhea: Modern. I like. How about sermons on You Tube and you can post confessions on the priest's Facebook wall?
Me: ROFL. What about you? Are you religious?
Rhea: Voodoism
Me: Fancy! Do I have a voodoo doll yet?
Rhea: I'm making one. It takes time
Me: Lol. As long as it's good looking!

Another potentially awkward moment is the first meeting. Pictures can only tell you so much. When you talk to someone over an extended period of time, you tend to create a mental image of them in your head. This leads to a very nervous moment right before you actually meet. What if your mental image of how a person feels like, of how you feel with them, is wrong?

Rhea and I finally met at Starbucks.

"Hey, so this is how you look like in real life." She then followed with an afterthought. "I thought you were taller."
"Umm. Ya." I wanted to tell her that I thought she looked much slimmer and ask whether she photo shopped her pictures but mumbled out a polite "nice to meet you too."
"So."
"So.. Coffee?"
"Tall non-fat mocha please," she said to the barista. She then turned towards me, "Would you like one too?"
"No. I don't like mocha."
"Umm… Ok."

We chit chatted awkwardly for some time. But we just didn't have the same connection that we had online. Our mental images were way off. Sometimes you can have great chemistry over the phone and the Internet. Yet when you physically meet, there's nothing.

More importantly, however, she was not kidding about the voodoo doll (It was decent looking though). I was glad she wasn't interested. I did not want to find out if what they say about sticking pins in voodoo dolls is true. Perhaps this was a different kind of beginners luck. She decided not to put a pin through my voodoo doll.

Meeting someone and realizing there's no chemistry is a risk you had to live with. But, in some kind of twisted karmic logic, this was perhaps a warning to heed an important lesson. It becomes hard to separate what's a joke and what's real when you are not talking face to face. Different people interpret wit differently. Finally, I learnt my lesson and decided to turn down the humor.

After a couple of months and a number of interesting experiences, I had also come to an important conclusion which I shared with Ru

Ru: Hi bro

Me: Hey! Sup?

Ru: Sitting in the parent's room. They say hi

Me: Hi back

Ru: So how's meeting women going?

Me: It's not that bad

Ru: Good. Find anyone yet?

Me: No

Ru: Oh. Can you hurry up? The sale season is coming soon and I'd like to go shopping for your wedding

Me: My wedding?

Ru: Well my clothes. Of course, you'd like your only sister to look pretty at your wedding

Me: I thought I was adopted

Ru: It's ok. I will overlook that

Me: You are so sweet

Ru: Thank you. Thank you

Me: So I've realized that there are two kinds of people on the website. One kind is in the more traditional mold. They have a certain set idea of their requirements (for the most part) and are looking to get married in a short space of time

Ru: Ok. And the other kind?

Me: Well, The other kind is the more casual one. This kind may or may not have certain checklists, but are looking to spend time getting to know someone before making the big jump

Ru: And?

Me: I've realized I fall into the latter category

Ru: Oh!

Me: I think this is going to take some time. It takes a lot of time to really get to know someone. So you might have to wait for a little bit before you go shopping crazy

I expected a big backlash or at least a few stern remarks as I said that and waited for her to communicate the conversation to the parents. To my surprise, my parents were quite comfortable with the idea.

Ru: Mom's saying that 'Beta, making the right decision is more critical than making a quick decision. We just wanted you to get the process started. You should take your time.'

Me: Nice. Cool!!

Ru: But I am not falling for your BS. I'm shopping anyways and sending you the bill ☺

Me: What have I done to deserve you?

Ru: You must have been very good in your previous life ☺

I guess that's what makes Indian families so special. For all the drama we like to create and surround ourselves with, when the right moment comes, we shed our petty arguments and differences, and come together as one strong supportive and cohesive unit.

Perhaps it came at the right time as well. As luck would have it, by spring of 2009, certain other things were becomingly increasingly important.

3 Uncertainty

Sometimes we choose the road we follow.
And sometimes the road chooses us.

Growing up my parents frequently read me the story about the ant and the grasshopper. It went:

"It was a warm summer month. Winter was about to come. The ant was working hard to store food for the winter when it would be too cold to find food. She saw a grasshopper that was busy singing and lazing in the sun. The ant stopped "Friend grasshopper, the winter is going to come soon. Why don't you stop lazing around and start collecting some food to store for the winter?" The grasshopper ignored the ant and went along its merry ways. Soon winter came and it was harsher than usual. The wise and hard-working ant survived the winter on the food it had stored. The grasshopper, who had fritted away its time in wild abandon, died of starvation."

My parents loved telling me this story at bed time. They felt that it would teach me the value of hard work and moderation. That lesson did stick with me. For 28 long years.

In the summer of 09, as the financial crisis deepened and the economy plunged, I learnt that there was a different ending to the story that was never told to me. That summer, it seemed that the grasshopper got all of the ant's food, the ant died, and the grasshopper survived.

My sister came online that night. There were no hellos; she went straight to the point.

Ru: So we saw in the news that the Dow crashed. They said some big company called Lehman failed and someone called AIG was taken over by the government
Me: Yes. It's quite unexpected. No one expected it to be this bad
Ru: It's bad out here as well. Dad saw this article in the newspaper about people losing their jobs
Me: Layoffs have started at most companies. A few of my friends got laid off
Ru: Oh! You should be safe? You don't work on Wall Street. Chicago is far away from New York
Me: Well, let's see. Almost all sectors are laying off right now

After a pause, I figured I'd rather tell them the news now than have them find out about it indirectly.

Me: They announced a 20% cut a few days ago. Should find out soon
Ru: Don't worry! You'll be safe. You work hard and you're smart
Me: Supposed to be random
Ru: Oh! Mama is saying not to worry. Have faith in God. She'll go do parsad at the Gurdwara tomorrow
Me: Sure. It's not that bad. 1 in 5 chance
Ru: Ok! 20% isn't that bad
Me: Yup. It'll be fine. Going to sleep now. Gnite
Ru: Bye bro. Dad says he'll wire you some money tomorrow
Me: I'm good. Don't need any
Ru: Just in case

A 20% chance of failure, and conversely, an 80% chance of success would be considered good odds in a wide number of things. Ask any gambler; he would be happy to play those odds. But the thing with odds is that they never really represent the human condition that well. For someone who is unfortunate enough to be in this 20%, the outcome is pretty binary.

For the first 20 years of my life, I had lived at home. For the last 8 years, I had stayed away from my family. Initially, this self-imposed exile was for undergraduate studies at a US university. Then, when a bachelor's degree didn't seem enough, it expanded to graduate and business school. The rationale was that putting in the effort and hard work towards a good education would enable me to have a comfortable well-paying job and a successful career. That did happen. After finishing business school in 2007, I landed a well-paying job at a consulting company. The work was interesting, allowed me a few luxuries, and still have enough left over to save some money and pay off my student loans. I put in the extra effort and long hours to show I was a good worker hoping to make my future more secure. That did happen as well. Soon, I was promoted and my life seemed to be on the right path.

However, by the winter of 08, the world began to change and things started to slow down. By summer of 09, we were in a full blown recession. Nearly everyone was cutting back. So was my employer.

Two days before the announcement I decided to catch up with an old friend. One of the reasons was because I hadn't seen him in a while. But the bigger reason was that we shared a similar background and he always had an interesting insight or wise words to share.

Deepak was from Delhi and had a typical upper middle class upbringing. He moved to the US about 10 years ago for higher studies. After graduating, he stayed back to work on an H1-b. With the global recession, his consulting firm was cutting back as well. There was much in common in our backgrounds. I figured a chai-latte with him would be more rewarding than a coffee with one of my American friends.

"Hey! Long time man!" I said as we shook hands.

"Too long," Deepak replied. "I was travelling for over a month. Just got back into Chicago."

"That's a lot. Where did you go?"

"Texas. A client in Dallas."

"Summer in Dallas could not have been fun. It's hot like India." Deepak nodded.

"Back on the beach?" I asked.

"More like permanent beach now."

I was stunned. Beach was euphemism for bench in the consulting world, the time you were not working for a client. I thought to myself, 'Did he just tell me he got laid off?'

"They did a 30% cut yesterday," Deepak shared. "Pretty much everyone on the bench."

"Man! I'm sorry to hear that. I thought being on a project made you secure?"

"So did I. Heard a rumor that they had to do it before the quarter ended to shore up the earnings projection."

For a lot of people near their 30's, layoffs were a new concept. We had missed the tech collapse, and the world had been pretty rosy since.

Deepak then moved to one of his more philosophical moods. "The way things are being done is ironical. They make such a point about spending money on employee development, training, team building and the sorts. Then one day you are called into the office and told your services are no longer required. At least my manager was decent enough to not give me the whole story about the economy going bad and company needing to cut back, and was straight up. Poor guy! They fired him after he fired us."

I nodded my head in agreement. "I'd probably not want to hear someone trying to rationalize it. So what next?"

"No idea. They gave a 2 month notice. I had my green card in process. I haven't spoken to the lawyer so far. But what people told me is that I have to find something within 2 months or go back home."

"How's the girlfriend handling it?"

"So far she's been ok. We had our two year anniversary two weeks ago and I was thinking of taking it to the next level. But, an unemployed guy popping the question. Not quite sure about that."

"Let me know if I can help. I'd forward your resume, but we are having a round next week as well. Got my fingers crossed."

"All the best man. You know, growing up in India, we all had been taught that perseverance and hard work were the secret to a success. But now it seems that it is a world where hard work and dedication matters little. You're just a profit-loss equation and have little control over your future."

"True. Everything is uncertain and it all comes down to a game of chance."

"Anyways, enough of this depressing stuff." He then changed his face to a serious expression and leaned forward "So, tell me?"

"Yes," I said, anticipating something important.

"So when was the last time you had a beer?"

I laughed. "Let's go."

As we headed to the bar, I wondered (I probably shouldn't have), "So do you think you are ready to go back home?"

Deepak replied with a cryptic answer; one that I'd only understand months later.

"I don't know. Maybe it is time to go back home. Or maybe it's too late now. Let's see how the dice rolls."

Toby's Journal
Entry 35, 2009

Uncertainty is a temptress. We may try our best to avoid her. But what is certain is that at some point of time, she will find us. The only question that remains is whether like Medusa, she will paralyze you, or whether like one of the nine muses of ancient Greece, she will drive you to greater things.

We all strive to have a sense of stability and consistency in life. Moments of uncertainty are considered dark. What we fail to see is that we are in fact byproducts of these dark uncertain moments. From the time a sperm, one of thousands, runs an uncertain race to the egg, to the moment of birth where a delicate infant leaves its safe cocoon into an unknown world, it is, in fact, the basis of human existence.

It's not just our being; this muse has the power to shape the paths we take through our story. The greatest achievement of mankind has come not through stability, but through doubt and uncertainty. What motivated the earliest ancestors to wonder what more they could do with two rocks except to have them just lying around? Or what motivated man to chart a path to moon except the uncertainty brought about by a powerful foe? She nudges us to reach into our very depths and examine what is important, what can be possible, and what dreams may come?

Uncertainty is a temptress we all meet. If we chose to embrace her, she is the beautiful muse who shakes us out of our mental cocoon, and urges us to ask *questions that really matter. Or if we chose to fear her, she is the terrifying Medusa who will paralyze our every thought and action.*

-X-

For me the layoff had created precisely such an opportunity of uncertainty. A moment where I was suddenly knocked from a stable steady cruise. A moment where if I chose, I could see a bouquet of possibilities or a jungle of fear. A moment where, like Deepak, like countless others, I could ask the right question. A question that really mattered.

To keep my mind of things, I kept myself busy with mundane tasks over the weekend. Sunday night was spent rolling in the bed and finally falling asleep. Monday morning, the decision was swift. There were four of us in the team. We knew one had to go. We did not know what the criteria were. But that Monday morning, all of us were prepared. I thought I'd feel nervous. But what I really felt was a feeling of relief. It was a path I had no choice over.

At 9:30 a.m., I saw the director make her slow walk towards our cubes. She passed me and stopped by my coworker's desk. There are moments when nothing is said, yet everything is crystal clear. By lunch, my co-worker had left.

I phoned my parents and let them know I was safe. They were elated. For me the emotion was bittersweet. That the uncertainty of the past few weeks was over was definitely a relief. But that moment had left an indelible impression. Like a muse, it had forced me to become aware of greater things, to perhaps ask the most important question facing my life.

Was it time to return home?

4 Reminiscences

We capture your memories forever.
(Eastman Kodak Slogan)

My life used to have very few questions. Most of them revolved around where to go for dinner and what to have for dinner, which at the time seemed somewhat important. Now, they had been replaced by a new set of questions, which made the previous questions look minuscule.

All the uncertainty around the layoffs had made one question become increasingly important. The geographical question of where to have dinner was replaced by a life choice. Should I stay in the US or return to India?

But it wasn't a simple question. It was a penultimate question, the answer to which depended on the answer to many more questions before it.

At the same time, talking to prospective partners had also exposed a new set of questions. The preference question of what to have for dinner was replaced by what is really important to me. When you try to open a window into yourself to let someone take a peek inside, you can't help but stealing a glance yourself and discovering new things. Combine these two, and you open up a Pandora's Box of questions concerning your very existence. What do I really want? How do I get there?

On the face of it, these questions appeared simple enough. Truth be told, the fundamental questions of life always remain simple. It's the answers and the ease with which they come that changes. Since Deepak was the one who was partly to blame for this whole line of thought, I met up with him for coffee to share the big news.

"Hey," I greeted him.
"Hey! How's it going?"
"Good, you?"
"Taking it easy. How were the layoffs?"
"Survived."
He gave me a high five.
"Did you figure out your green card thing?" I asked.
"Yep," he smiled. "It was in the last stage, so I'm good. Just going to relax for the next few months. Spend some time with the girlfriend."
"That's great," I congratulated him.
"So you all set then? You should be good for at least a year now that the layoffs are done?"
"Yes and no. It kind of got me thinking."
"And…?"
I dropped the bomb.
"I'm thinking about moving back."

He made a funny expression, the kind you have when you are both confused and surprised but not sure if you are more confused or more surprised.

"Why?" he asked.

We spent the next half an hour discussing my thoughts.

"So how did you come to this decision?"

"Well, after spending a lot of time thinking, I put my life into four buckets.

One was the Love bucket. Things that were important.

Two was the Hate bucket. Things that were disliked.

Three was the Indifferent bucket. Things that were not important.

And lastly, the Regret bucket. Things that I wished I had put some more time in or done differently."

Deepak nodded. "Seems fair, bucketman."

"What I concluded was that a lot of personal and professional goals have been achieved. But, every achievement had a cost."

Deepak raised an eyebrow. "Costs?" he said, rubbing his thumb on his index and middle fingers.

"Yes. Friends. Family. The one thing that bothers me a lot is how it has kept me away from my home and my family for so long."

"Agreed. That is a cost we all have paid."

"But what bothers me most is that things still aren't settled. Does it really make sense to slog it out for the six years that it would take to be a permanent resident? What if there was another recession and I get stuck with no choice but to move back? What if my parents fell sick and I had move back? What if I got settled and my wife and kids could not move back?"

"It's a valid question, but it isn't anything new. You are being fearful of a lot of hypotheticals."

"I don't think so. I think it's being realistic. The world is different from when I had left my home 10 years ago. India has grown so much. I hear about so many possibilities and growth."

He wasn't impressed with my argument.

"So when were you last in India?"

"3 years ago."

"That's a long time. Longer in India years. India has changed a lot. Things change in months now. People have changed and are changing. Attitudes are different. Also, did you consider that having stayed here for so long, your viewpoint has changed as well."

I cut him off. "It's still my home. I can adjust."

"It's a big decision. It's a different country now."

One of the things that made Deepak interesting and entertaining (for the most part) was that he loved telling stories to make a point. So, it wasn't a surprise when he decided that I needed to hear a story to understand his point.

"I read a story once. A man spent his entire life searching for the Truth. He looked everywhere and could not find it. Finally he decided to go to the Himalayas and look for the Truth. After days of meditation, a lady appeared in front of him. She said, 'I am Truth. Now you have found me.' The man was shocked. He said, 'How can this be? You can't be Truth. How can I tell everyone that I found Truth and she is old, wrinkled and white haired!'".

Deepak paused for effect and then continued "The old lady said, 'then go tell them that you found Truth and she is a beautiful young woman.'"

"And your point is?" I asked.

Another thing that made Deepak interesting but a bit eccentric was the unique and memorable way in which he expressed himself when he got into one of his philosophizing moods.

"My point is that the moment we are in, the circumstances and expectations we have, all have a profound impact on how you perceive something and the path you take. The founder of Greek tragedy Aeschylus said that 'there is no greater pain than the memory

33

of joy in present grief.' Right now, all the negativity surrounding you has the potential to impact your perception and decisions. There's a version of India that you remember. It may or may not be the version you go back to."

I wasn't convinced and I didn't feel like having a long discussion on it. "It's my home," I said forcefully. "I am certain my friend. You are not talking me out of this one."

Deepak sighed. "I guess we all have to make our own discoveries in our own ways. Three years is a long time to be away. Do you have PTO days left?"
"About two weeks. Why?"
"Well, instead of making a rushed decision, why don't you take a two week vacation? It will give you a perspective of how India is now. It's not a big delay in the grand scheme of things, right?"

I had to concede that he had a valid point here. "That's not a bad idea. I don't get paid for unused PTO days anyways if I quit. I could do some advance networking."
"Sounds good. Don't get me wrong bro, I am not saying that you are right or wrong. I will be sad to see you go. But I'll be happy that you have found what you really want. All I am saying is that it's a big decision. Take your time. Maybe you'll feel differently in a month."
"I know. I value your opinion, which is why I'm here."
"I should start charging you." He then paused, leaned forward and said with a serious expression. "So tell me…"
"Yes? I said sheepishly. I had heard this before.
"When was the last time you had a beer..?"
I laughed. "Let's go."

As we walked to the bar, he took out his phone and showed me a picture of him with his parents in India. He then mused, "You know happy memories are like blurry old photographs. When times are tough, it's natural to seek comfort in them. And nothing is more satisfying than the memory of growing up. Memories of loved ones.

Memories of home. But the question is, do you spend your time trying to recreate those blurry old photographs? Or is it all about creating new ones that become blurry old photographs you cherish?"

Toby's Journal
Entry 41, 2009

Home is never a simple image. It is many images, many photographs in an album.

I wonder what made home 'Home'.

Was it the rush to get to school in the morning, which no matter how much you planned always ended up in a last minute dash?

Or was it the fact that once in a while you could pretend to get sick, and get away with not only taking a day off but also being pampered and treated like royalty by your parents and grandparents?

Or was it the constant jumping over the fence to retrieve the cricket ball while trying to escape the gaze of that crazy dog, one of which, every neighborhood seemed to have?

Or was it taking the extremely long route home in the evenings to avoid the old Mr. Sharma, who insisted on lecturing you that your cool new Pink Floyd album need not be blasted and shared with the whole block?

Or was it the fragrance of freshly made pakoras and tea wafting through the evening air that you barely got to taste because you were told to be a good kid and wait for the guests to finish, leaving you hoping that they didn't devour everything?

Or was it spending starry nights playing stupid childhood games while waiting for the electricity to come back as your parents tried desperately to manipulate a draw so that you and your sibling didn't fight at the end?

Or arguing over the TV remote, or complaining about the choice and quality of food in the house, or brooding over demands that you expected your parents to meet but were not met, or....

At that time, all these things were annoyances. Our lives would have been so perfect without them.

Who would have believed, that years later, they would become cherished memories that always brought a spontaneous smile.
Who would have believed, that years later, these photographs would be the fondest memories that we had earned.

-X-

Most photographs are transient.

They fade away.
They get blurry.
They get lost in time and space.

But a few always come along that make that elusive jump to remain in our memory; forever etched in our hearts.

Almost ten years after leaving India, the memories of home were driving me to make the biggest decision of my life. Ten years later, they were becoming photographs that I was trying to recreate.

PART 2

5 Perfection

What makes the desert beautiful is that somewhere it hides a well.
(Antoine de Saint-Exupery)

Toby's Journal
Entry 44

The single puddle of muddy water on the parched
broken field;
The solitary sparrow using it to shield her chicks
from the summer heat.

The bare leafless tree trying to stretch towards the
sun;
The unrelenting dew, reviving itself every morning
awaiting new green leaves.

The incessant dance of hide and seek choreographed
by the moon and the clouds;
The fleeting lonely beam of moonlight that penetrates
to illuminate the dark night.

Reality is, Hope and Despair lie in the same places.

And they're just a matter of perspective.

What changed my perspective, was her.

-x-

The last few months had, to say the least, been quite taxing. The layoffs had led to many extremely important questions and very few answers. As I engaged in my quest of soul searching and realigning my long term goals, my understanding of myself and my goals changed dramatically.

I had mentioned to Deepak that I was trying out a matrimonial website. One rainy day in November, he called to see how that was going.

"So how's matrimony.com coming along?" Deepak asked.
"It's going. Definitely not priority number one, but not completely stopped as well."
"I never understood how those websites work. I always wanted to try them out, but now the girlfriend would skin me alive if I went and created a profile."
I laughed. "Believe me it's not the best place to meet anyone. I was excited in the beginning. So many possibilities.."
"Then?"
"Then reality happened. Once in a blue moon, I find someone interesting. Things start well. Then the chemistry or attraction fizzles. If that work's then something else would happen."
"Something else like? She'd only tolerate and marry you if you'd pay her a bribe of a million dollars?"

41

"Your jokes are getting worse. It's like she'd say something or do something unexpected, or I'd say or do something unexpected, and poof! The bubble bursts."

Deepak laughed. "So my friend, you are finding quirks. Little insignificant things that are immaterial, but we make them important."
"Well it is a big decision."
"Good luck with that. How long have you been on now?"
" Many many months."
"And how many profiles have you gone through?"
"Probably a gazillion."
He laughed. "And nothing yet?"
"Well no. But there is a silver lining. It's helped understand my needs and expectations. I know more about myself. I know more about the right fit.."
"So many profiles and no one you feel getting close to. I think you are looking for an oasis in a desert."
"No. I'm just looking for perfection."

With my life in a state of flux, and minimal expectations from the website, there were many moments when I came close to deleting my profile. Many thoughts flowed through my head. Perhaps now was not the right time. Perhaps I needed to take a break from the pressure of getting married. Perhaps I'd meet my true love at an after work happy hour in a crowded bar. Perhaps I'd randomly bump into her while trying to catch the train back home. Then sanity would prevail and instead of deleting it, I'd hide my profile for a week. You don't really make connections at an overcrowded bar. And a moment where you randomly bump into someone while trying to catch the train only happens in *Bollywood* (all though I wouldn't complain if it was followed by a hot woman in a small white dress dancing in the rain).

Finally, there was the Indian in me. I had paid a small fortune for the website. I should use it until the subscription ends.

I'm glad I did.

With a few days left on my subscription, I wasn't expecting to initiate anything new. I was happy to let the subscription run out and close my account. This was just me window shopping at work.

And there she was.

I'm not really sure what initially attracted me to her and made me click her profile. There was just something different about her. Was it her unconventional user ID? Was it the picture with a genuine infectious smile and a childlike twinkle in her eyes? Or was it the fact that this was the first time I'd seen someone describe themselves as being happy in their profile?

I had to say hello.

(Hello!)

3 messages

Toby Arora TobyArora31@gmail.com
To: C@gmail.com
Fri, Nov 21, 2009 at 12:10 AM

Hi C,

This is Toby from matrimony.com. Thought I'd drop a quick note to say hello. Slow day at work and Friday afternoon is probably the least productive time for me. Can't wait for the weekend to start!

I noticed we have a few things in common including a passion for traveling. Have a long list of places I'd like to visit but hate traveling alone. Have you traveled much?

And I think we share an interest in law as well. I was considering doing a degree in corporate law at one time. How do you like what you do?

Anyways, I really liked what you had to say about yourself and am looking forward to knowing you better. I've rarely bumped into people who'd describe themselves as happy. Pretty cool!

Toby

C C@gmail.com
To: Toby Arora TobyArora31@gmail.com
Sat, Nov 21, 2009 at 9:35 AM

Hi Toby,

What took you sooo long? I've been waiting for 29 years.

Just kidding! I am a bit excited about this weekend and that's overflowing into everything else. My best friend is visiting from North Carolina. I haven't seen her in years. We studied Law in India together and then went to North Carolina to do our LLM. After graduation, she decided to stay back in the US, while I decided to come back to India. Things were changing so fast in India and I did not want to miss out on all the action. So I packed my bags 3 years ago and became a part of corporate India.

What about you? What's your story? Where did you study? Any best friend who was a doppelganger through your journey?

Taking about journeys, yes we do share a few things in common (interest in law, passion for travelling). I've backpacked across Europe and that was the best vacation of my life. If you haven't, you should try that as soon as you can. I also took a few road trips all over the east coast while I was in North Carolina. My next destination is South America, which has always been very very high on my list. What about you?

I am sure it's going to be an interesting journey knowing each other. I am soo glad you haven't adopted the bio data approach. It gets boring.

As for being happy, that's how life should be. It's too short to be anything else. There are ups and down, but if you keep your sense of humor, life's a breeze.

But for now, what works best for you?
Chat? Email? Skype?

Or let destiny take its course?

Toby Arora TobyArora31@gmail.com
To: C C@gmail.com
Sat, Nov 21, 2009 at 10:51 PM

Haha.

The bio data thing I don't get. My parents sent me a bio data of a girl once and it was almost like a resume and nothing about the kind of person she is. It sounds like a business transaction. And if that's the basis for anything I wonder how things would turn out.

Well I didn't go to a cool school like you (I'm warning you, I'm not that bright!). I went to University of Virginia and Penn State, which when I was home in Chandigarh earlier this year, got me a few blank stares.

We do have a similar story about realizing that things are changing so fast in India and wanting to be a part of it. So I do have to make an important disclosure and I think it should be upfront. I am currently contemplating moving back to India (Bombay in fact) in Feb. It's been one of those decisions that has been lingering for a while now and I have given myself a deadline on it. I am not sure if you have a specific checklist, or are looking for someone in the US; but if you are, then I shouldn't be wasting your time and you can ignore the rest :).

In terms of what I am looking for, I don't really have a checklist. I've realized you never know who you have chemistry with. Long term, you probably want someone you can be best friends with and mentally in sync as well.

So since we are leaving the rest to destiny, how about telepathy?? (ok sad joke. sorry). Skype hasn't been working for me. I need to get a new laptop, which will happen next week. Phone's good. I'm at 31213131. Send me your number and I'll give you a call. Also am on google chat most of the time as well.

Toby

Perhaps the most important thing I felt I needed to be upfront about was the move that I was contemplating. Everyone has different preferences and priorities. Why waste time and effort (mine and hers) if that was an immediate disqualifier?

Once I had shared that important disclosure, I braced myself for a quick decline. I didn't expect us to bump into each other on Google talk a couple of hours later.

Day 2
November 22, 2009

Chat with C@gmail.com

C: Hey!

Me: Hello. I just sent you a loong email

C: Yes I just read it

Me: and?

C: So, item 1 (I like bullets): Checklists. I don't really have a checklist. I'm just looking for someone well-educated, affectionate, and ambitious. Someone who I can share my life with and have no regrets

Me: Cool. I don't have one either. Chemistry can come from anywhere

C: Ok. And now item 2: Location

Me: The big one…. (insert suspenseful music here. Dead ant, dead ant, dead ant dead ant dead ant)

C: Dead ant? Oh I get it. You get zero points for humor. Having lived all over the world, I think that location is immaterial. Location doesn't matter the person does. To me if we click and you decide to move to India that probably works out better for me. I'm close to my parents and the US gets a tad bit too far

Me: Nice. I am refreshed to hear that. Normally that's unsettling for most

C: Where in India are you from?

Me: Chandigarh

C: I love Chandigarh!!!!! It's one of the cleanest places in India

Me: And very beautiful too

C: Planning to move back to Chandigarh?

Me: No. I think the opportunities still lie in the bigger metros. I am contemplating Mumbai or Delhi. A bit biased towards Mumbai

C: Good choice. But the weather can get tricky. Ever been?

Me: Plenty of summers. I have a few relatives that I used to visit. It's been a few years since my last trip

C: Few years is a long time. India changes every year now

Me: So I've heard

C: So why Mumbai over Delhi?

Me: Two reasons. One, it helps when you have family and friends around. Two, I think it presents better career opportunities

C: I just realized I don't know what you do ☺

Me: Haha. I work for a consulting company with their strategy practice

C: Sounds fancy

Me: Yes. Glorified presentations and excessive number crunching.

C: "Glorified presentations". Lol. I can relate to that. I work as a corporate lawyer for a multinational FMCG firm

Me: Sounds like fun. Do you ever regret moving back?
C: Not at all. To be fair, there are some obvious differences between life here and there. But things in India are changing
Me: Changing for the better!
C: I think the best decision I made was to move back to India after my LLM. More growth, better job satisfaction, small luxuries you will never have in the developed world, closer to home, and after all, it's your own country
Me: I'm glad to hear that
C: Are you close to finalizing a decision on relocation?
Me: Decisions are hard. They should have laid me off. Would have ended up with a nice severance and the decision would also have been made
C: Hahahaha. Sometimes it's easier if life makes the decision for you
Me: Much easier. I plan to stick around till January. There's a decent year-end bonus that I deserve. Thinking about taking that and quitting.
C: Makes sense. So are you a quick decision maker or do you take time?
Me: I like things to be spontaneous. But you have to mix and match. The move decision has taken months. It's a big decision. It's good to evaluate and consider all possibilities. But you have to be careful you don't fall into the over thinking and overanalyzing trap.
C: Decisions are hard indeed. Hey going to do a quick tea run. Brb
Me: No problem

So far so good, I thought to myself, as I made a quick run to the fridge for a Diet Coke (no this isn't a product placement). She was back in less than five minutes.

Me: That was quick
C: Yes. I'm fast. So Item 3 (see I made a list).
Me: I see that
C: Did I mention I have a very good friend at work who studied at University of Virginia as well?
Me: Nice. Who?
C: Karthik Das
Me: Small world. He was a TA while doing his PhD in one of the classes I took
C: This is such a small world. Are you still in touch with Karthik?
Me: Been a while. Are you going to do a background check now ;)? He probably won't remember me
C: I am sure he would :)
Me: I hope he doesn't. I remember almost dozing off in his class. Not sure if he would have good words about me
C: Now I shall do a background check on you tomorrow
Me: Ok. After that, I don't think I want to find out what item 4 on your list is
C: Haha. That's the big one. Item 4

Me: It is?
C: Yes.
Me: And...?
C: Item 4
Me: What is it??
C: So Item 4 is that I have to go now
Me: Lol. I was actually waiting for something big
C: I got you there. Unfortunately, as much as I liked talking to you, I have to get some work done pretty soon
Me: No worries. Let's talk tomorrow then
C: Sure
Me: Phone ok with you?
C: Good. Should I mail you my number?
Me: Probably. I'm not good at guessing numbers :)

Day 3
November 23, 2009

I was surprised how well our first conversation had gone. There was none of that typical awkwardness that is characteristic of initial get to know conversations. It was fluid and both of us seemed to be at ease with each other. We joked and we discussed some serious topics. We talked about the past and we talked about the future. It seemed like we had known each other for years. She had definitely piqued my interest, and perhaps, there was some potential here. I had Monday off and was excited and looking forward to call her up talk over the phone.

"Hi! Can I talk to C?" I asked.
"C speaking."
"Hey! This is Toby."
"Hey Toby. How's it going?"
"Going well. How are you?"
"Good. *Acha* Can I call you back in 20 minutes when I get back home?"
"Sure. No problem."

It was around lunch. So I figured I'd have a quick bite since 20 minutes typically turn into an hour Indian time. She called back exactly 20 minutes later.

"Hey Toby."
"Hey! How's it going?"
"Good. I'm sorry I couldn't talk to you earlier. I was coming back from a wedding."
"No problem. I'm impressed. I was expecting it to be 20 minutes India time, not exactly 20 on the dot."
She laughed. "I can hang up and call back 20 minutes later, if you'd like that. Act pricey and all."
"So much for giving someone a compliment."

"Just kidding. You know I really liked talking to you yesterday. It was effortless and laid back. Normally, I get a volley of questions, most of them pointless, and then I feel like I'm being graded and judged."

"I can start interrogating you, if you'd like that," I said in a mock serious tone. "Let me open up Excel and make a model of compatibility. Then act stereotypical male and all."

"So much for giving someone a compliment."

"Just kidding. No, I really liked talking to you as well. It's like talking to someone you already know. So how was the wedding?"

"Tobyee!. So many aunties. They all eat your head. Same stupid questions and unwanted advice. 'When are you getting married? You should settle down, it gets harder the older you get. We know someone who knows this guy. Why don't you meet him?'"

"Haha. That must be fun. I hate that whole aunty nonsense. First they pull your cheek or mess with your hair, then they joke about something embarrassing from your childhood, and then give you a lecture. Sometimes I feel perhaps my parents pay them money to come harass me."

"Not my cheeks, no way. Well at least I got good food out of it. Had the most amazing chicken tandoori."

"Chicken tandoori. That's my favorite. Did you get me some?"

"Stole it in my purse. Should I mail it to you?'

"That might take time. It's lunch all ready. Now I'm going to have something less interesting."

"What are you having for lunch?"

"Spaghetti noodles with traditional Indian flavoring, with peas and carrots," I said, trying to sound sophisticated.

"Oh. Maggi," she answered.

"*Sahi Jawab*. You guessed it right. Maggi with yoghurt."

"Maggi with yoghurt?" She screamed. "What normal person has that?"

"They go well together. Balances the spice out."

"I've never heard that one before," she laughed. "You really are unique."

51

"You should really try it, one day," I said in the most convincing tone I could muster.

"No thanks. I'm never taking culinary recommendations from you."

"Your loss."

"It's ok. So, any plans for the day. You have most of Sunday left."

"Well not much. Some friends were making a plan to watch this movie. It's a copy of this English movie called Hitch. It's supposed to be funny."

"Partner? That's an old movie. It's got Govinda in it. I never saw it."

"Good guess again. It's not good?"

"No idea. You know how Govinda movies are."

"Brainless. But that's what I like about them. They are hilarious."

"Haha. Don't tell me Govinda is your favorite actor."

"You didn't know that," I exclaimed. "He is awesome. I think I'm going to redo my whole wardrobe based on his style."

"Orange pants, Fluorescent green shirt, White shoes, multi colored scarf with big polka dots."

"That's how I dress for work! You must be psychic!"

She laughed. "You are a really interesting character, Toby"

"Character?" I asked with a surprise.

"Yup. I think that's what I am going to call you."

"Character?" I asked with a greater sense of surprise.

"Yup. Toby the character. Totally suits you."

"Fine. I'll think up a weird nickname for you as well then."

"Try try. Nothing can beat 'character'."

I never ended up watching the movie Partner. Time flew by so fast, we only realized we were talking for 6 hours when the first rays of sunlight started streaming through her window. We quickly said our byes. By Tuesday morning, I was eager to chat with her again and logged on to Google Talk via my iPhone.

Day 4
November 24, 2009

Chat with C@gmail.com
Tue, Nov 24, 2009 at 9:05 AM

C: Hey character
Me: Character? Hey chikni
C: Haha. Where did you find that word from? Looks like you are practicing for moving back to India already. You'll fit right in if you talk like that
Me: Lol. Good to know. Well I have to come up with a counter to character. Now just need to learn how to whistle
C: Yaa. That will complete your skill set. Then you'll be a proper character
Me: Lol. Ok I guess calling you chikni didn't make you stop calling me character. I'll think of something else
C: While you think, I talked my way out of a ticket today. So proud of myself
Me: How?
C: This cop caught me crossing a red light. Was taking out his *chalaan book* and telling me 'Madam you are going to get a 2000 rupee ticket.'
Me: Pricey! How did you get out of it?
C: My car is slightly banged up in the front. So I made a crying face and told him that papa doesn't even know I took the car and then I had an accident that banged up the front. He's going to be angry as it is but with a ticket he might throw me out of the house
Me: He fell for that?
C: Little bit. I even shed a small tear
Me: Tears on demand. I shall remember that
C: Oops. Shouldn't have told you my secret skill. So, then some loafer on the street teased this girl by calling her chamiya and she started shouting at him. So he told me to not do it again and went to sort out their fight
Me: Hehe nice. Lucky you. Maybe he was calling chamiya to you?
C: eeeeeeeeeeeeeeeeee! No!! It's cheap and sounds bad.
Me: Perfect. You call me character, I'll call you chamiya
C: Whatever. I don't care. It doesn't affect me
Me: Lol. Fine. We'll stick with chamiya then
C: Fine. I don't want you permanently damaging your brain trying to think of something else

Day 5
November 25, 2009

(Good Morning!!)
2 messages

C C@gmail.com
To: TobyArora31@gmail.com
Wed, Nov 25, 2009 at 7:19 AM

Hey Character,

Good morning....I am sooo sorry I missed our chat date.. I caught a cold and wasn't feeling too well.

How was your day at work? I am finishing up with a conference call and stealthily sending you an email. Will log on as soon as I am liberated from work!

Talk to you soon!!

CHAMIYA

Toby Arora TobyArora31@gmail.com
C C@gmail.com
Wed, Nov 25, 2009 at 8:07 AM

Haha.

You like the word Chamiya, don't u?

Sent from my iPhone

We spoke a lot during the next few days. And we spoke about a variety of topics; some relevant and some completely nonsensical. We spoke about the present, the past, the future; our hopes, aspirations and expectations. Serious topics never really felt serious or made us feel pressured. Almost all our conversations were littered with laugh and play. Soon I was beginning to think what had been previously unthinkable.

Maybe I had finally found that elusive chemistry that I had been so desperately searching for.

Maybe I had found perfection.

6 Intoxication

Maeve: She who intoxicates.
(Gaelic)

Toby's Journal
Entry 47, 2009

The moon came and replaced the evening sun, only to be replaced again at the break of dawn.

The nightingale went quietly to her star specked abode, only to return to her sweet melody in the morning.

The dew arrived with the cold winter night, only to be driven away by the morning sun.

Every day, the cycle of time revolves around the same cosmic dance.

However, for us, this cosmic dance had no relevance. Time for us began to be measured by moments when we spoke, and moments when we longed to speak again.

Have you ever noticed dew drops falling from a leaf? It sits on the edge, very slowly extending itself, a long eternal moment. Then suddenly in a blink it falls and vanishes. And then you wait, impatiently, for the next one to slowly trace its path towards the edge.

When we were speaking, it seemed like a long eternal happy moment.

When we stopped it seemed like it had been a blink, a small vanishing second.

When we were waiting to talk again, it seemed like a never ending impatient delay.

-X-

It was surprising how we got so close in such short a time. Neither of us had such an instant connection with anyone before. Neither of us was in any sort of hurry to find an instant connection. In fact, neither of us considered ourselves to be predisposed to being the kind of people who meet someone and instantly develop chemistry with them. Yet there we were.

Both of us spent more than a few moments thinking about the pace, and whether we should slow down. But by the end of week 2, we were inexorably intertwined in each other's life.

Day 15
December 5, 2009

Chat with C@gmail.com
Sat, Dec 5, 2009 at 8:31 AM

C: Hey Character
Me: Hey Chamiya
C: What you doing?
Me: Just got up and am now watching TV. And talking to this weird girl on google talk
C: Aww. Don't talk to a weird person. ….. Why are you talking to her?
Me: Well it's called earning good karma. You know, community service. Someone has to talk to her
C: Ignore. Maybe you like talking to her?
Me: Hehe. Ok. I'll be nice to you. I guess I probably like talking to her. She is quite interesting
C: :) Toby the character gave me a compliment. He likes talking to me Yipppieeee
Me: Lol. How's the cold?
C: I think I'm still loopy from all the medication I've been on
Me: You sound more fun with the medication
C: Shut up. I am an incredible amount of fun all the time. And btw, your name rhymes with *dhobi*
Me: How astute. By the way, I have good news. I'm planning to make a quick trip to India in late December/early January
C: Subtle topic change. But that is good news! How come?
Me: Well a couple of us were planning to go to UK for new years. Now that plan is cancelled, because a few friends can't make it. So… since I had already paid for my ticket, I can use that towards a ticket to India Plus, I figured I'd network a little bit to get a job in India
C: Oh! I thought you were coming to see me
Me: Well. That too. ☺
C: To be honest, you should come in the first 2 weeks of January because it'll be an effective period for interviews. Try to schedule a few interviews before you come. It's a slow process here
Me: That's what I am thinking as well. My ex manager moved back to India. So I'll reach out to him. Then, have a few friends who might be able to help
C: Cool. Be careful though. They try to lowball you thinking you don't know about the Indian market
Me: Same all over the world, no?

C: No. They can get really dirty here. I had a friend who was jumping with joy when he got a 12 lac package. When he started working, they took out 1 lac for a laptop and 50K for office expenses

Me: That's sneaky. Even if you trick me into such a job, I'd either leave or do such a crappy job

C: This is India, not America

Me: Well. I heard they announced a 7.9% gdp growth. It can't be that hard to get something good

C: It's probably because last year wasn't so great. I just wrote about that in a brief

Me: Practicing work on me?

C: Hehe. I just finished the brief and sent it to my senior. See, even with all the distraction you cause

Me: Distraction? I'm entertaining you and keeping you motivated, so that you can write a better report

C: India is still so much about seniority. I did all the work and research, but my senior gets to argue the matter

Me: True. But I think that's how the legal profession is all over

C: Lol. It's strange na. We haven't even met, yet we share so much

Me: Strange it is

C: I hardly know you. Yet I feel like I know you

Me: Maybe we should ignore each other for the rest of the week?

C: You are mean today. Try ignoring me for a week. It's a challenge

Me: Lol. That might not work out too well

C: Exactly!

Me: Ok. How about ignoring you for a few hours? I'm going to go back to sleep. It's criminal to be up at 8 am on a Saturday. Call you?

C: I was going to say no and tell you to go ignore yourself. But since you are bribing me with a call, I will allow you a few hours of sleep after that

Me: How magnanimous of the Chamiya! Give me 5 minutes

We spoke many times over the next few days. She was like fine wine. The more I spoke to her, the more intoxicated I got with my attraction. What endeared me more was that we were also turning into the best of friends, sharing almost every detail of our life. So when Deepak, who was busy enjoying his sabbatical learning more about his girlfriend, called on a Saturday night wondering if I had had some beer lately, I was eager to meet up and share the exciting new person in my life.

And that night, after a few more beers than usual, I also ended up blurting some personal thoughts over email.

Day 16
December 6, 2009

(no subject)
2 messages

Toby Arora TobyArora31@gmail.com
To: C <C@gmail.com>
Sun, Dec 6, 2009 at 1:05 AM

You know what bothers me about you???
You're so perfect.
And I've never thought I'd find someone so perfect!

Sent from my iPhone

C C@gmail.com
To: Toby Arora TobyArora31@gmail.com
Sun, Dec 6, 2009 at 8:03 AM

You just made my day!!!

C

And half a day later…

(No more compliments??)
9 messages

61

C C@gmail.com
To: Toby Arora TobyArora31@gmail.com
Sun, Dec 6, 2009 at 12:41 PM

What happened? Why are there no more compliments in my inbox?
Please go have some drinks and then write me sweet-sweet emails.

Toby Arora TobyArora31@gmail.com
To: C C@gmail.com
Sun, Dec 6, 2009 at 1:53 PM

Yes. Poor me had to come into work, with a hangover (and slightly embarrassed). I doubt drinking at work will go well with the boss.

Here's an idea. How about you be sweet to me and I'll be sweet back?

C C@gmail.com
To: Toby Arora TobyArora31@gmail.com
Sun, Dec 6, 2009 at 1:56 PM

I am always sweet to you Character. I'm sweeter than sweet n low.

C C@gmail.com
To: Toby Arora TobyArora31@gmail.com
Sun, Dec 6, 2009 at 3:09 PM

And now I am missing talking to you.

Toby Arora TobyArora31@gmail.com
To: C C@gmail.com
Sun, Dec 6, 2009 at 3:18 PM

Aww, cuteness wants to compete with a sweet n low packet.

In a meeting but will be done soon. Should I call you?

C C@gmail.com
To: Toby Arora TobyArora31@gmail.com
Sun, Dec 6, 2009 at 3:32 PM

My phone is in my parent's room.

Email will have to do tonight.

Toby Arora TobyArora31@gmail.com
To: C C@gmail.com
Sun, Dec 6, 2009 at 3:39 PM

Haha. Me thinks that me should call your phone and wake up your parents....

C C@gmail.com
To: Toby Arora TobyArora31@gmail.com
Sun, Dec 6, 2009 at 3:53 PM

And when my dad says hello in his scary Amrish Puri voice and asks angrily which duffer is calling his daughters phone in the middle of the night, what are you going to say??

Toby Arora TobyArora31@gmail.com
To: C C@gmail.com
Sun, Dec 6, 2009 at 4:00 PM

I will do my best SRK imitation; say I'm Raj and ask for Simran.

Day 20
December 10, 2009

(Hey)
I message

C C@gmail.com
To: Toby Arora TobyArora31@gmail.com
Thur, Dec 10, 2009 at 1:43 AM

Hey Toby,

I know it hasn't been long since we've met each other. But we've become so close that it seems much longer. It's just so wonderful that we have such amazing chemistry. It just feels so pleasant when you know you have someone to start the day with and look forward to ending the day with.

Soo, I just wanted to tell you that you are someone special. And even though you torment me with your horrible jokes, I just can't wait to finally meet you in less than a month

C

Strangely, even though we hadn't met, and had only known each other for a few weeks, both of us had started to like each other. A lot. My closest friends had already heard stories about how awesome she was and how fascinated I was with her. So had her friends. It just seemed right.

As shocking and unexpected the pace was, barely three weeks after meeting by chance and getting to know each other, both of us felt comfortable talking to our parents that we were considering someone seriously.

That weekend, I went first.

Day 22
December 12, 2009

Chat with C@gmail.com
Sat, Dec 12, 2009 at 9:05 PM

Me: That was a really sweet email you sent
C: I thought that I'd be nice since you are always complaining that I'm not nice. On the contrary, you're never nice
Me: I'm never nice?
C: No
Me: That's a blasphemous lie
C: Is that supposed to sound more convincing because you are using a BIG word?
Me: Yes
C: I'm convinced. You are so virtuously right
Me: *ignored*. Nice profile pic
C: Lol. Thanks
Me: You're wearing green
C: You're not color blind. Yippee!
Me: Lol. This is what I get for being nice. Sarcasm
C: :p
Me: You're dress reminds me of a *bhindi*
C: A *bhindi*. A Ladyfinger. An Okra. I remind you of a *bhindi*?
Me: Umm. Yes
C: Why?
Me: Well, cause you are so skinny
C: I like being skinny. And I'm not skinny. I'm hot
Me: Oh! Fever?
C: Oh! Shut up
Me: Oh! So tell me?
C: Oh! What?
Me: When it gets really windy, how do you stop yourself from flying away?
C: Dork! I tie stones to my feet
Me: Must be a lot of them?
C: Hanji. Ten kilos
Me: Oh!
C: So much crap from the fatso. Sir *bakwaasalot*! And what's with the 'Oh' fetish
Me: That's because I have news, and I was going to tell it in your style 'Oh! I have news!'
C: Then I might stay. Unless you are going to compare me with another vegetable.
Me: I booked my tickets

C: Oh cool! I'll forgive you for the infraction earlier. Did you tell your parents or are you going to surprise them?

Me: Well I had to tell them. They would have gotten a heart attack if I walked through the door

C: Not that you have great sense of humor, but it's way off tonight!

Me: :P I'm going to stay with my uncle in Bombay. So had to tell them. Also, wanted to tell them about you

C: and…

Me: And what?

C: What did they say?

Me: Told me to get my brain checked.

C: What did they really say Character?

Me: They're pretty excited

C: Cool. Are they ok that I am bit older?

Me: Yes

C: You know, that could be an issue, right? Generation gap and all

Me: No they are cool. But you are right on that

C: On what??

Me: There is a generation gap. Thats true for everyone, right? At times, there might be some opinions or values that can clash

C: True. That can happen in both sides

Me: But we have similar values and expectations and understand each other. I'm sure we can manage our families if something comes up

C: I totally agree, Toby. It takes a lot of effort to create something beautiful. I'm glad we're on the same page

Me: Great. Btw, another piece of good news. I got a few meetings set up. Some very senior people. So hopefully things should move fast

C: That's great! Congrats! You know I have a feeling it might take long. You shouldn't rush it. Make sure you find the right opportunity

Me: That is possible. There are many people considering moving back. Remember I told you that during our first conversation. You're talking to someone who's temporarily unsettling himself

C: I know. I just want you to know that you shouldn't rush it because of me. If for some reason, your move takes a while, I'll visit you after you come here

Me: I don't think moving back home should be that hard. But I'd prefer to get something in hand before I quit my current job

C: Ya. Don't leave the security of what you have. You'll be in a better bargaining position

Me: True. Sometimes you can plan things in life. Sometimes it's about a moment when a decision feels right. Let's see how it turns out

C: Ok. I just want to let you know that if we're together (I really hope we will be) I will support you in all decisions you make. I am just not there because of

what you are today… but because you are a great guy… who will get a lot of success… and along the way if there are any hiccups we will face them as 'one'
Me: That is so sweet. I appreciate that
C: Ok enough serious talk Character. When you coming to Mumbai? I get back on the 2nd
Me: Jan 9 to 24. Most of it in Bombay.
C: OMG! How can I tolerate you for sooo long?? I will be traumatized!
Me: Tolerate? I can make my visit shorter so that you have to tolerate me for less
C: No. It's ok. *Theek hai, kar lenge.* I'll manage to tolerate you
Me: Acha? Sure?
C: Hanji. Social service
Me: Haha. My joke on me. You are getting smarter
Me: I feel like having Okra now
C: I doubt a *bhindi* would taster better
Me: Really? How many okras have you made out with?
C: Kick

Day 26
December 16, 2009

Later that week, she went second.

Chat with C@gmail.com
Wed, Dec 16, 2009 at 10:23 PM

C: Hey fatso
Me: Hey stick
C: So I told my mom about you at dinner
Me: And
C: And nothing
Me: Nothing? She didn't have a reaction.
C: She did
Me: Which was?
C: Nothing
Me: Stop playing or I'll start calling you an okra again
C: What a threat! But first you have to thank me
Me: Why?
C: I had to lie so much for you
Me: Why?
C: I couldn't find anything good to say about you. So I had to improvise
Me: Really? What did you improvise?
C: Well for starters. The pic. I was going to show her your pic but then I thought of the the reaction she might have
Me: My pic should have a good reaction. I look good
C: You live in a fantasy world, don't you?
Me: So what did she say?
C: She said you looked good
Me: See
C: I did show her some other guy's pic though
Me: Other guy? Good. Go talk to the other guy
C: Sorry baba. No she was happy that you were well-educated
Me: Good
C: She was also happy that you were moving back
Me: Sure? I was fearful that might unsettle your parents.
C: Nope
Me: Sure

C: Yes. Trust me. I have it under control. She's just happy to hear about a boy. Any boy

Me: Any boy? That's supposed to make me feel better?

C: Oops. Teehee

Me: Anyways, I got an interview setup with a bank today. But they don't seem to be paying too well

C: That sucks! Come soon

Me: Why?

C: Because I miss this dork. And the thought of this dork makes me happy

Me: Acha. Are we still talking about the other guy or me?

C: Yes. A bit too much wine for dinner

Me: I'm glad they don't make those. So where are we meeting?

C: I don't know. You're the guy. You should plan.

Me: All I know in Bombay is Juhu Beach.

C: That'll be a cheap date. What will I eat?

Me: Lol. We'll get you some pav bhaji at Juhu beach.

C: You eat that. Let me find you a girl who will eat pav bhaji and coca cola at juhu beach and then step into the dirty water with you wearing a bright red chamki sari. Then u guys can splash dirty water at each other. Perfect date. Should I look for one?

Me: If I go date someone else aapka kya hoga? Someone has to make the sacrifice to date you for the good of the human race.

C: Now, I need to find someone for you

Me: That does it. I'm dragging u to that dirty beach

C: I am not coming with u. I don't wear saris... I don't eat pav bhaji and I will never step into the filthy water

Me: Ok. Lemme cancel my India trip

C: Stop threatening. I'll come but I have conditions. You have to put parachute hair oil on our juhu beach date. and orange pants....green shirt????

Me That's it?

C: And those huge Nike sneakers with that blue tick sign

Me: Nikki sneakers it is

C: Yes that's how you should pronounce it. How come Toby the character is losing the battle. Toby is losing Toby is losing

Me: I'm not losing. Ok how about something more pleasant like a meal of delicious grilled salmon and red sangria, on a table floating on a platform in the middle of a crystal blue lake, with musicians on a separate platform playing music, and a not too distant waterfall emptying into the lake, enveloping the area with a light mist of cool vapor, all surrounded by different hues of green

C: Sounds romantic. How sweet. But I don't eat fish

Me: So much for trying. It took me twenty minutes to come up with that. Maybe I should just throw you in the water

C: I don't know how to swim. If I drown, my parents will call the cops and get you thrown in jail

Me: Don't worry. They will probably reward me for taking care of their problem
C: And what are you going to do after I drown?
Me: Maybe I'll throw you in the water and then save you
C: Ooh. So that's how you plan to woo me? Throw me in the water and then save me so that I'm indebted to you for life. And then I say '*Ab to mujhe Toby se hee shaadi karnee padegi!* I have to marry him cause he saved my life.'
Me: Yes. There you go. Small problem though. I don't know swimming
C: You should learn. Otherwise how will you become the hero?
Me: True. Maybe I need a different tactic. Know any goons for hire?
C: Lol. Find them yourself. So we have a date?
Me: 10th Jan. 6 Pm. Juhu Beach

One of the rarest and most beautiful things in this world is to meet someone who has the ability to intoxicate you. Every moment with her was exhilarating, and every moment without her was spent captivated by thoughts about her. She was like the finest of wines.

And I was getting drunk.

7 Puppets

Those are strings, Pinocchio

"The problem with getting drunk is that eventually there is a hangover," Deepak said as he ordered two more shots of some weirdly named shot. He'd recently spent 2 bucks to get a new iPhone app that listed a thousand different kinds of shots. After making this stellar investment, his new goal was to try his best to maximize the return on his new acquisition by making me try out the most arcane obnoxious sounding shots he could find.

"So why is the solution for my heartbreak to drink more?" I inquired.
"Because, right now you're going to be too drunk to be sad about what happened."
"And when I wake up?"
"You're going to be too busy cursing me out for the hangover to be sad about what happened."
"And when the hangover is gone?"

"We will come have more shots. This app has a 1000 different shots. We still have 990 to go."
"9-9-0," I repeated slowly.

There are two golden rules to having a great time while drinking:

1. Never argue with a drunk.
2. Never argue with a drunk when you are drunk.

I decided to adhere to the second one.

A few more shots later, Deepak started to philosophize.
"The one thing in life we always tend to under appreciate is how fragile the nature of our reality is; how delicate those strands are from whom suspend our beliefs and our reality; and how little it takes to break one of those strands and throw our reality into a chaotic spin."

"Is that supposed to make me feel better?" I said. "I'm too wasted to even understand what you are saying. I'm not even sure how you are saying something so complicated after having had so many shots."
"I forgot I was speaking to an intellectually challenged individual. I am saying let it go. *Khao Pio, Aish Karo.*"

I pretended to ignore his remark on my intellectual prowess. "and let everything pass?"
"Maybe it was meant to be that way. Maybe she overanalyzed and got confused. Maybe she meant to say something else and got stuck in the emotions of everything. Point is, you can't let something you have no control over bring you down." He turned around to speak to the bartender "Four shots of Goldschlager please."
"Well true. Not much I can do about it. What bothers me more is that it came out of the blue."

"I agree. I have to admit I am surprised as well given how well you two were getting along." He paused and asked. "What about India plans now?"

"Tickets booked. Going to go."

"Any leads on the job front?"

"Some. People find it hard to take it seriously that I want to move back. They say once you come, we'll talk."

"Well I have a friend who works in Private Equity. I'll let him know you're coming."

The bartender placed four shots of a clear liquid with floating gold colored specks in it on the bar table. She still hadn't cleared the glasses from our previous shots and the area looked like a mini graveyard of empty shot glasses. Deepak got off the wooden bar stool (and in the process almost toppling it over), picked up two shots and motioned me to pick the other two.

I mumbled a spontaneous string of questions. "What are those specks floating in the shots? Where are we going? And....why do we have four shot glasses?"

"Those my dear friend are actual 100% real flakes of Gold. We put them on mithai. The Swiss put it in their alcohol. I figure you need some good surprises."

By now we had walked up to two beautiful brunettes who were sitting on the other side of the bar.

Deepak beamed "Ladies, my friend here just discovered this amazing shot that has 100% real flakes of gold in it. And he accidentally ordered four. Would you like to try it?"

Walking up to random women in bars was typical Deepak. But the shot was surprisingly refreshing. However, the real surprise had come less than 24 hours earlier when I had received surprising news from C.

Chat with C@gmail.com
Fri, Dec 18, 2009 at 10:45 PM

C: hey Toby
Me: Sup?
C: not much

After a few minutes:

Me: How was your day? You sound very quiet
C: No
Me: Ok
C: Yes, I've got some bad news. I need to be in Calcutta starting early Jan for work. So don't know how we are going to meet. Maybe we could try something in Chandigarh?
Me: That's disappointing
C: I know
Me: Are you sure its work and you not losing interest?
C: No its work. I said I am willing to come down to Chandigarh
Me: That's really disappointing. I made my plans centered around Bombay
C: All right

This was a big disappointment. I didn't really want to deal with it that night while I was still in a bad mood. I told her I'd give her a call in the morning. But when I opened my inbox the next day, I was in for a shock.

(Good morning)
4 messages

C C@gmail.com
To: Toby Arora TobyArora31@gmail.com
Sat, Dec 19, 2009 at 9:21 AM

Hi Toby,

I will try my best to meet when you are here. However, after thinking about the situation, I am also concerned that your move to India will take time and it will take you time to settle down here.

This might not be the most appropriate time for things working out.

I wanted to share that since it's been bothering me. Let me know what you think about it.

Thanks,

C.

Toby Arora <TobyArora31@gmail.com>
To: C C@gmail.com
Sat, Dec 19, 2009 at 9:42 AM

Hey,

This isn't something new that just came up. I am not sure what exactly is bothering you here. If you can be more detailed, we can talk about it.

Sent from my iPhone

C C@gmail.com
To: Toby Arora TobyArora31@gmail.com
Sat, Dec 19, 2009 at 10:24 AM

Hi Toby,

I'll be more detailed.

1. The move is going to take time. You will be busy interviewing and this might turn out to be a process that takes time. So the move will take time on your part.

2. I think being outside India for so long, you are underestimating how hard things are here. I think you are assuming a lot and are not completely aware of the downside.

To be honest, I don't know how much we can achieve together in the short term. There are too many loose ends.

So I am sorry Toby...maybe I am telling you this too late in the day but when I really thought about it properly, I don't' see this working out.

I had a pretty bad hangover the next morning. But Deepak was right. I was more bothered about the headache than actually mope over what happened. I also was beginning to understand his remark about how we tend to under appreciate the role of chance in our lives. Moving was a big decision, and a lot of things could take time. Perhaps her situation had changed and she couldn't afford to wait. Perhaps she was interested in someone else now.

It wasn't that her heart had changed that bothered me. It was that things were going so well that it was just completely unexpected.

One day you can have everything figured out and be in control, and the next day you are back to being life's puppet.

Toby's Journal
Entry 51, 2009

Maybe our reality is a puppet. A puppet suspended with thousands of strings we call beliefs and expectations, that shape our everyday lives. And when these strings don't move for a period of time, we create for ourselves a cloak of our invincibility; and then intoxicated with this newfound illusion, conveniently forget those strings ever existed.

Then one day, someday, a moment comes.
A moment we never anticipated. A moment which we refused to consider because we were invincible.

When this eventual moment of truth comes, it shatters those strings of beliefs and expectations. Everything we knew, and expected, is now in a state of disarray. All that is left is a sense of wonder, 'What just happened!?'

And then you hear a voice saying,

'Those are strings, Pinocchio'.

PART 3

8 Tranquility

Akath katha prem ki,
kuch kahi na jaye.
Goonge keri sarkara,
bethe muskaraye.

Inexpressible is the story of love,
It cannot be revealed by words.
Like the dumb eating sweets,
Only smiles, the sweetness he cannot tell.

(Doha's of Kabir, a mystic poet in 15th century India)

Tamil tradition holds that in ancient India lived 7 great Hindu sages. It is said that to these sages was made a divine revelation that they then recorded on palm leaves. On these leaves they wrote down the past, the present, and the future of all humanity. These leaves survived thousands of years and the bulk of them still exist to this day. They are called the Nadi Leaves.

To get a Nadi leaf reading is a relatively simple exercise. A learned man takes your thumb impression and matches it to the corresponding leaf. Once the right leaf is found, it will, in a cryptic way, tell you the most important parts of your existence.

My Nadi leaf reading said many interesting things. The one that struck me most was when the pundit told me that around the age of 30 a great lesson will start to reveal itself to me near a body of water. It struck me more for its vagueness than for the charm of a great revelation. Standing in the lobby of The Radisson, next to a tranquil lake in Powai, who would have guessed would be the start of a profound discovery.

The hotel lobby was quite busy. The black couches in the center of the lobby were all taken by what appeared from the brightly colored saris and an over abundance of gold jewelry to be a small marriage party. There was a well dressed security guard standing next to them who seemed a bit out of place. I snickered. Perhaps his purpose was to guard all that gold jewelry. I eagerly scanned the other end of the lobby.

There she was.

I walked up to her to say hello.

She was wearing a cute brown leather jacket and pair of jeans. "So this is what you look like in real life?".
"Yes. How do I look?"
"Turn around. Let me check you out."
"Idiot."
As we walked to the restaurant, I fumbled a compliment.
"So you look more beautiful than I thought you did."
"Thank you. Let's go to the restaurant before it closes. I'm starving!"
"Sure".

"Ummm, where's my return compliment?" I sheepishly asked as we walked to the restaurant.

She laughed. "Return compliment? This is not a birthday party Mr. Character, where you'll get a return gift, if you give someone a gift."

"Remember all the discussions that we had about how you should be sweeter to me?"

"Yes. But then it'll become boring. No fun if there isn't a little drama."

"Little?"

"Shut up. Table for two please."

A neatly dressed man, with a thin long moustache greeted us.

"Hello Sir, Hello Madam, Table for two. Very good. This way please."

He excitedly took us to our table. And by excitement, I do not mean the normal show of excitement to make you feel welcome. By excitement I mean the uber excitement you see when two long lost friends bump into each other. I'm not sure if he was genuinely happy to see us or if he had been told that the best form of customer service is to jump for joy and be overly happy. We smiled to each other as he enthusiastically blurted out the specials.

"I'll have the chicken sandwich, cooked in olive oil," she said.

I ordered pasta, to which he gave his seal of approval with an 'Excellent choice, sir.'

"So my choice isn't excellent?" C asked him.

The smile vanished from his face. "Oh certainly madam.

Much better than sir's choice," he quipped with a big smile.

Now, it was my turn to give him a long hard stare.

"I will get your drinks," he mumbled, and quickly rushed off.

We hadn't ordered drinks yet.

We spent a few moments enjoying the hilarity of the situation wondering what our mystery drinks would be, and it helped alleviate the initial nervousness we both had.

"So, how was your cab ride? Did you have any trouble getting here?"

It had indeed been a long and winding journey to get to this point. We had stopped talking after the unfortunate email exchange. One night, we bumped into each other on Skype.

C: Hey Toby, Do you have a minute?
Me: Why?
C: I think somehow you misunderstood me
Me: How so?
C: Please hear me out. Look at it from my perspective. You come to India to visit we hang out and click. Then your move takes time or you settle for something to make the move faster. I get stuck right. I don't break up because I like you. Plus pressure on me to get married
Me: I can get that maybe after you spoke to your parents, they had a rethink or chose to be over cautious. But it's your decision as well
C: I know but we will also be in a situation that has a lot of uncertainty. What do I do then?
Me: Life is always uncertain. I had told you about moving back much earlier. In fact, because we had talked about it and you seemed so cool about it, was one of the main reasons I let myself get attached
C: Ya. But it is something that makes things difficult
Me: It's not impossible. You know, what bothered me most was the way it was said, and that instead of talking about it, I got a 'please be informed' email
C: Maybe my way of saying things was inappropriate. I am sorry for that

In life, we all have these moments of failure. Moments where we lose perspective and do or say things we don't mean. Or moments where we over analyze or over think a situation, and start imagining a reality that is more a product of our fears than of facts and probabilities. The more we talked, the more we began to realize that it was one of those moments of failure. That the days we had spent not talking to each other had been miserable for the both of us. That it was up to us to believe in a beautiful future together and give it our best shot.

Our friendly waiter came back with our order. Apparently he had spent the last twenty minutes trying to find a way out of the situation he had got stuck in, and peppered us with his memorized statement.
"Excellent chicken sandwich, in olive oil, Mam."
"Excellent pasta, Sir."
Satisfied with himself, he proudly beamed, "Both very excellent choices!" and left.

She excitedly dug into the sandwich.
'This chicken sandwich is my favorite," she said after finishing a bite.
"Why?"
"Why? Coz its sooo good."
"Hmm." I said, making a face.
"What's the face about?"
"Nothing."
I got a threatening look.
"Well it just that the poor sandwich looks kind of sad. I wouldn't want to eat such an unhappy looking sandwich."
I immediately got a kick on my shin.

The lunch lasted for two hours. We decided we needed a change of location and decided to get some coffee and sit by the pool.
"First impressions?" she asked. "Am I like you thought I would be in real life?"
"Well you seem a lot like the way I imagined you," I replied.
"And how did you imagine me?"
"Like the way you are."
"How am I?"
"Sweet."
"Really. How can you tell in less than 2 hours?"

I thought about it. "You're right," I apologized. "How about a kiss and we can figure out if you're sweet or not?"
She blushed. "No. I think I'll settle with me not being sweet."

It was getting late. We decided to make plans for the next day.
"So what are your plans for tomorrow?", I asked.
"I have work. But I can get out early. What about you?"
"I have to meet this headhunter around lunch. Nothing much after that. A lot of people seem to still haven't come back from their New Year vacation."
"Ya. A lot of people took days off because 1st was on a Friday and it turned into a long weekend. Even my office is half empty. Most people will be back by the 11th."
"I guess. So let's meet for drinks then, and maybe catch a movie after that."
"Sounds good. I'd get bored talking to you anyways."
"Hmm. Proof that you are not sweet."
"I am," she emphasized, while putting on some lip gloss.
"No. Remember we agreed earlier."
She laughed. "I like raspberries."
"Random. Why?"
"I just do. My lip gloss is raspberry."
"I've never had raspberries. Are they sweet?"
"You can find out."
"Ok. Give me your lip gloss."
She threw the lip gloss in her bag. "Nope."

Half an hour later, I dropped her off at her place.
"You know, It was really nice to meet you," she said.
"Same here."
"I might decide to tolerate you."
"Works for me."
She gave me a hug.
"Here's something to remind you of me tonight."

Monday, Day 2 in Mumbai

Monday morning was jam packed. So was the afternoon. We ended up speaking in the evening.

"Hey. Busy day. How was yours?" she said.
"Well woke up late and was still jetlagged. And then had to rush to my meeting."
"That sucks. Did you make it on time?"
"5 minutes late."
"Oh. It's India. 5 minutes is normal. Fashionably late."
"Ok. So how fashionably late are you going to be today?"
"Not that much. Why don't we do the movie first and then do dinner. What time is the show?"
"Cool. I'll see you at the theatre at 6."
"Ok. What movie?"
"Umm.. It's a surprise."

We met up at the movie theatre. She was on time. I was late (fashionably). We rushed to watch the movie.
"So why are we watching a scary movie?"
"It should be good. I heard it's really scary."
"I don't like scary movies. I get scared."
"I thought so."
"Then, back to my original question: why are we watching it?"
"I figured you'd get so scared that you might decide to hold me close and I could sneak in a few hugs."
"Dork. I am going to sit three seats away."
"Suit yourself."

The theatre was empty, except a few couples scattered in the corners and the occasional warm aroma of *samosas*.
I sat in a chair on the corner. She went and sat three seats away.

After a few minutes, she asked "So, aren't you going to ask me to sit next to you?"

"Nope. Don't shout for me when you get scared."

"Idiot!"

Eventually we compromised. I moved two seats, she moved one.

The movie was slow to start with. "Did you figure out what raspberry tastes like?" she asked.

"Nope."

"Maybe I should show you," she said playing with the lip gloss in her hand.

I held out my hand for the lip gloss.

She came and kissed my lips.

After the movie, very little of which we actually saw, we drove to Bandra to have dinner at an Italian restaurant. The place was tastefully done, with intricate stone statues, and huge decorative jars filled with olive oil, colorful pasta and bright red chilies. In a corner, there was a grand old tree nestled against a small pool and a sprinkling of yellow autumn leaves adorned the marble floor. We sat next to the pool under the moonlight.

"So what was the movie about?" she asked as the waiter brought out a bottle of red wine.

I winked. "No idea. I was distracted."

"My parents will ask. I have to figure out something to say."

"Go home and Google it."

"You're useless. Did you do anything productive all day?"

"I was very productive. How was your day?"

"Very busy. There's this big presentation coming up. Everyone is going back and forth on the PowerPoint. One person adds a line, another takes it out, and the third asks where it went?"

"Normal corporate life."

"Yes. But I get stuck in the middle. No fun for me. Any who, how was your day? Any progress?"

"Progress? With?"

"Headhunters?"

"Oh. That. I think it went good. He was definitely impressed by my education and experience. He asked me why I was looking to move back. I told him the reason and my desire to be closer to home. Then we discussed pay expectations and role preferences. Left on a good note, he said he'd circulate my resume and I should expect to hear from him soon."

"So not bad. Did you do anything in town after that?"

"I met Shah. We studied together during my masters and he had come back to take care of his family business. He was super excited to hear I was moving back. Mentioned that this was the perfect time as economy was recovering and hiring was picking up."

"Cool. Seems like a nice guy."

"Yep. He offered to get me in touch with a few of his friends working at a senior level in consulting. Let's see if he comes through."

She affectionately touched my arm. "That sounds good. I hope it works out well character."

"Cheers to that." We raised our glass to toast.

Time just flew by and it took a couple of times of the waiter asking us if we'd like something else before we realized we were one of two couples left at the restaurant. It was well past midnight when I dropped her back at her apartment.

As she got out of the car, she said "You know it's hard to describe how you make me feel."

We didn't need words. Our smiles said it all.

9 Pursuits

Life is about chasing butterflies.

Tuesday, Day 3 in Mumbai

My phone rang early Tuesday morning.

"Good morning."

"It's 7 in the morning," I complained

"I know. Helping you get over your jet lag."

"How thoughtful of you. You do realize I am technically on vacation."

"You're welcome. My parents were still awake last night."

"And…"

"My mom asked me if we two got along."

"And.."

"And I told her I liked you."

"And… their reaction?"

"Nothing. She was happy. They want to meet you now. Your parents as well."

"Cool. Well I'm here. Anytime they want to meet works for me. In terms of parents, you guys are welcome to come down to Chandigarh when I'm there. Or even if I'm not, they can meet later."

"Sounds good. Mom was asking how the job thing and moving timeline is going to look like."

"Well you know about the job thing. Moving, we can talk about. I'm flexible. Need a week or two to wind up. Are you in a rush?"

"Not really. All though, I'd like full 24 hour access to my character sooner."

"Good then. When are we meeting?"

"Late night coffee?"

"Done. You're buying."

"Cheapster."

The day went by pretty fast as I had a marathon session with a few recruiters. They came in different flavors. Some were serious and to the point. Some were laid back and friendly. Some were plain funny. One even considered me an oddity of sorts and was quite infatuated with my name.

"Is your name really Toby?" he asked for the third time

"Yes," I replied for the third time.

"Are you sure? Sounds like a nickname. I thought your name would be Tubvinder."

"Haha. You are a funny one."

At the end of the call, he asked again. "So Toby is really your real name then?"

"No. My real name is Ghansham Das."

C couldn't stop laughing when I narrated the incident with the recruiter later that day.

"You actually didn't tell him that, did you?" she asked between fits of laughter.

"I did. I was so irritated. People get stuck on funny things. What if he didn't like my hair?"

"You can have the job but please come to work with parachute coconut oil in your hair."

"I'd rather be jobless."

"So any other progress? You should try getting past the recruiters unless you meet more funny ones and have stories to tell after."

"Absolutely. I'm excited about tomorrow. I'm supposed to interview with this VP at an outsourcer tomorrow."

"That's great. Why didn't you tell me earlier idiot?"

"Just wanted to see your expression. And my friend came through as well. I'm meeting his friend. He's a senior manager at a MNC."

"Wow. Looks like it's all falling in place. My parents will be really happy to hear this."

Later that night, my parents and my sister called. They wanted to know how things were going. They had relaxed quite a bit when I had told them I was talking to someone. I suspect their plan had always been to set things into motion and then fade out and let things flow.

I told them things had been going great. I had made good progress at the career front. Things were beginning to happen and a move back seemed relatively comfortable. On the personal front, it was fabulous. We'd gotten along amazingly well, and it seemed soon we'd be considering the next steps. Life was good.

Maybe I had spoken too soon.

Wednesday, Day 4 in Mumbai

Wednesday was disappointing. I guess we all have bad days. I was due for one.

Manohar was a VP in a medium sized outsourcing firm. His office was peppered with pictures of him at various restaurants all over the world and his huge size was a testament to that. We had started off well. He liked my experience, was impressed by my qualifications and thought I'd get along well with his team. His clients were primarily in the US, so my experience was an added advantage. We were chatting casually towards the end of the interview.

"Where are you living in Mumbai," he asked.

"With family. I have cousin's here."

"Have you figured out a place to rent yet? It takes time to find one."

"Not yet. Depends on the job. I want to be close to work."

"Ok. So how was it like? It must be tough getting laid off, and having to move back so quickly."

I was surprised.

"Laid off," I asked after a moment of pause.

"Yes. That's why you moved back to India, right?"

Maybe I should have just let him believe that. But my instinctive reaction was to correct him.

"Actually, I am still working. I'm winding up and moving back later this month. As I said, I'll be ready to start by the end of the month."

"Oh. I thought you were already here. Excuse me." He paused and looked at his blackberry for a minute. He looked up from his phone. "Sorry I have an urgent email to reply to. It was nice meeting you. HR will get in touch with you shortly."

I felt that the interview had ended abruptly. I didn't have to waste my mind speculating for long. The HR person called later that day. He said apparently there had been some confusion. They thought I had already moved back and they couldn't make an offer as they couldn't be sure if I'd move back and it would take time. I tried to reason that I was all set to move back by the end of Jan which was the start date they were looking for. He didn't budge. In the end, as a sign of generosity, he added "Why don't you give us a call again when you have moved back?"

I was a bit disappointed by the outcome. C and I had spoken for a little bit after that. She provided some consolation. It's just a one off thing.

But this wasn't the first time that this had cropped up. I had heard that question a few times before. Maybe it wasn't a one-time thing. Maybe that's how it was. No one considered you seriously if you still had a job in the US.

Later that day, C called with a change of plans. "Dad's not feeling well. Can we cancel the coffee?"
"Sure. Anything major?"
"No. So, why don't we do dinner on Friday? You'd be done with your interviews as well."
"Works for me."
"Don't worry. Tomorrow will be better."
"I hope so."

Thursday, Day 5 in Mumbai

If Wednesday was bad, Thursday was a disaster.

It's perhaps some weird karmic irony, that exactly when you proclaim something special, the world turns around, and you realize you might well have spoken the complete opposite. It's as if suddenly, stars had changed in the night sky, and the world became a different place.

I was in a very bad mood when I spoke to C after the interview. "So how did it go?"

I had quite high expectations from my interview with Rajiv. He was a Director at a medium sized multinational and I had already had a few positive conversations with his senior manager who was a friend of Shah's. I felt this was the final screening before being given an offer. I met him at his office. He was a tall thin clean shaven man with a slight stoop. You would probably pass him on the street and not notice him at all. But what made him stand out was the obscenely loud parrot green bow tie with yellow diamonds on it. I managed to resist a smile. I just recalled that the senior manager had been wearing a bow tie as well. I had never really owned or even considered owning a bowtie. But if that's what it took to be successful in his kingdom, I was prepared to take the plunge into fashion oblivion.

"So my manager thinks you have the right skill set but I was confused as he mentioned that you haven't moved back yet?"
"I am in the process," I replied honestly. "I had two weeks of paid time off. So I decided to take the opportunity to visit and interview ."
Rajiv stared at my resume. "Are you sure you are moving back?"
"Yes sir." I explained that I was excited about starting work in India in Feb. I had already ended my apartment lease, and was ready to give my one week notice when I went back.

"So did you guys speak about anything other than moving back? C asked.

"Well yes and no. It was mostly downhill since the start. Most of the time he was probing me about my decision to move back. But he also raised something new. He was concerned that I had limited work experience in India."

"Well, you still have many transferable skills. You grew up here. It's not that you are a foreigner."

I made an audible hum. I didn't want to sound negative to her so I made one of my ill timed jokes. "Yes. On the flip side, I won't have to wear a bow tie now."

"No time for jokes. This is serious business."

"Just trying to lighten things up."

We decided not to meet that day. She was occupied with work. I wasn't in the best of moods. When we spoke later that night, the topic was still the same.

"You should try harder." she said

"Well I am trying my best."

"But still. I hope you have some progress to show by Friday."

"Maybe it's not going to be as easy as a hand fitting into a glove. It might take time. I might have to start a bit lower than I expected."

"You mean less pay?"

"Probably."

She didn't say anything. I could hear a sigh.

"Let me figure things out. Thinking from a long term perspective, I'd rather have the right opportunity than a temporary benefit. Things are a bit hazy right now."

"Ok. It's late. All the best for tomorrow. Gnite."

"Gnite."

One of things that keeps you going when you live far away from home, is that at the back of your head, you have a strong belief. This belief is that if things don't work out, you can always come back home. And it won't be that hard.

Sometimes our beliefs fail us.

Toby's Journal
Entry 2, 2010

A friend had once shared a remarkable and beautiful interpretation of life.

He said that life was like chasing butterflies in a beautiful meadow.

Each person has their own butterflies.

For some it's a true love.
For some, it's a life or professional goal.
For others it's a hope for the future.

That what life is about.

Dreams, desires and everything in between.

Butterflies.

He had then summed up the essence of life in one long sentence.

The joy about chasing butterflies, is not the satisfaction that comes at the end, but the path that takes you there;

The irony about chasing butterflies, is that sometimes you'll get so lost in the chase, you won't realize that you're left chasing thin air;

But the agony about chasing butterflies, is that sometimes you will keep on chasing, hoping, that a butterfly would materialize out of thin air.

Maybe my friend was right.

Perhaps I was chasing a dream that was never there. I expected the move to be easy, for the pieces of the puzzle to fit into place with relative ease.

Maybe I had the wrong expectation.

Maybe I was chasing a butterfly that just did not exist.

10 Endings

Bart! With 100,000 dollars we'd be millionaires. We could buy all kinds of useful things… like Love.

(Homer Simpson)

Friday, Day 6 in Mumbai

Clarity came on Friday morning through an unexpected phone call.
"Toby. How are you? This is Shyam here."

I had worked for Shyam in the US and he was also a good friend. He had recently moved back to India to be closer to his parents in Bangalore. Before coming, I had sent him an email to catch up.
"Shyam, what a pleasant surprise. How are you?"
"I am good. How are you?"
"Good."
"So have you settled in? How do you find coming back home?"
"It's good. Very rewarding. You don't realize all the things you had given up until you come back."
"That's great. How's the job?"

"Job is good. It's lots of work but very rewarding. The culture is slightly different. It takes a while to get things done. But, you know people have the same work habits all over the world. They want to work less and get paid more."

I laughed. "That's true."

"So you mentioned you are looking to move back?" Shyam asked after some chit chat.

"Well. Trying. It's turning into a very difficult process."

"I can imagine. It was harder than I expected for me as well. So have you interviewed anywhere?"

I walked him through my experience so far, starting with the recruiters. I ended with what a HR guy had told me after a phone interview which he considered as friendly advice 'If you wanted to work in India, you should have never gone to the US.'

"Hahaha. You know you'll find all sorts of people here. Some would value your experience and skill set. Some would have a genuine need excellent local knowledge and connections. There's a diverse bouquet of opportunities and needs."

"True."

"But this comment you should just ignore. He probably just didn't like you."

"Didn't like me. That's really comforting."

Shyam then proceeded to tell me about his move to India.

"I was in a similar situation as yours. My parents weren't feeling too well, so there was a slight urgency. Eight months ago, the economy wasn't that well. A lot of people were looking to move back as well."

"I remember that. Were you looking for long?"

"Well I was looking for something in hand before I moved. It's expensive to set up a house, and I wanted some security before moving. Initially, I got the same response as you. 'Why don't you talk to us when you get here? We like your profile, but we will only give you an offer once you are here, bla bla.'"

"Any idea, why that is so?"

"Two reasons," Shyam explained. "One, as long as you have a job, you have better bargaining power. The recruiters know that fact. Two, which is more important, when the economy went down in the US, a lot of people started exploring opportunities in India. People got offers, and then never showed up. That's why, when dealing with expats, recruiters are extra careful, so as to not waste their time."

"That sounds understandable. How did you convince them?"

"I was referred by someone very high who vouched for my seriousness to move."

"So that's what I need. Friends in high places."

"Haha. Well you do have me. If you ever want to move to Bangalore, I'd be glad to have you on my team or refer you."

"Thanks. I do appreciate that. Unfortunately, I can't go anywhere but Bombay."

"In that case, here's what I suggest. I am confident you'll get something good. Don't rush it. You don't have family commitments, mortgages and all. Take your time. Come back. Take a month off, and look in a relaxed manner. That's how you will get something not just good, but excellent."

Shyam did have the right advice. I agreed with him, that the best course of action would be to move back and then look for something. It was important to consider the longer term and the bigger picture than compromise for any short term temporary benefit.

However, as logical as it sounded, it was a difficult decision to be comfortable with in practice. After all, a lesson that is drilled into every child in every Indian school is that a bird in hand is better than two in the bush.

We spoke for a little while. Talking to Shyam had indeed been helpful. Things were becoming clearer. The pieces of the puzzle were fitting in and a picture was emerging.

However, I still did not realize that this new picture would be so different from the one I had imagined in more ways than one.

"So you only spoke to Shyam all day?" she asked, as we spoke over the phone after lunch.

"No. I also met this family friend who offered to get me in touch with some senior people he knows. He thinks they'd be more receptive because they returned to India after studying abroad as well."

"You are more than halfway through your trip."

"Looks like it's going to be the long route back," I sighed. "I'm leaning towards taking a month off and making sure I have the right opportunity."

"Hmph," She didn't sound too overjoyed.

"Anyways, I will see you at dinner tonight."

"Ok. I have to hop on to a call as well. Bye."

I spent the rest of the day catching up with some friends. I had just gotten out of the shower in the evening when the phone rang.

"Hey Listen," C said in a slightly tense tone. "We have to cancel dinner".

"We are cancelling dinner? Why?" I was puzzled

"My dad can't meet today" she replied instantly

"Oh. I was about to leave. Why don't we just meet up?"

"Not tonight. Let's talk tomorrow. Ok?"

"Ok. Is everything all right?"

"Yes. I'll call later."

Saturday, Day 7 in Mumbai

C was scheduled to fly to Delhi late Saturday afternoon and I hadn't heard from her since our call on Friday night. I called her around lunch wondering if things were fine.

"Hey! What's going on? Is everything ok?"

"Just busy," she mumbled.

"Ok. What happened last night?"

"Nothing. Dad couldn't meet. He wasn't feeling too well."

There was a different tone about her.

"You sound stressed," I asked.

"No. Just have to get a few things done before I leave."

"Do those few things involve us meeting?"

"Sure. I can meet you on the way to the airport. Can we do coffee at the mall?"

"Sure."

The coffee house was in a brand new mall but neglect made it seem like it predated the mall by a few years. Most of the unoccupied tables still had half empty coffee mugs and dirty plates left on them. We navigated past the occupied tables and chose a table in the far corner. The server came and cleared the leftover cups, informed us we had to go order at the counter, and made half an attempt to clean the table.

"I have to leave soon. Things are very busy," she said.

"How come?" I asked with concern. "Your dad still isn't feeling well?"

She crossed her legs and leaned back, "Well. Here's the deal. I'll be frank."

As if on cue, her phone rang. She spent the next five minutes talking on the phone about an upcoming conference. After the call ended, she started again.

"I have to go soon. So here's what's happening. I cancelled the meetings because I thought you'd have something to show."

I was a bit surprised. "I would have liked to get something as well, but one week is hardly enough time."

"Well, I was hoping you would have something by now. In fact, we are getting a bit uncomfortable about you moving here."

"How so?"

'The job thing."

I was a bit surprised. "I'm educated. I have good experience. These things take time. I am confident him and me can sit down and have an adult conversation about it."

"Well true But the uncertainty is making me uncomfortable. What if it takes more time than expected?"

"It might. Moving back is challenging."

"The fact that it's taking you time to find something decent is making me a bit afraid. There has to be some security."

"It's only been a week. We've spoken about this before. I'm educated and experienced. It just takes time."

"It's taking too much time. What if you move back and it takes three months? I'm not sure if I can wait that long."

"That's a bit too long. Unlikely, but you can never say never."

"Maybe your dad can help?"

"I told you. I'd like to do it on my own. Finding the right thing is more important for me than finding something fast. And I really am in no hurry about taking any steps before I get a bit settled."

The phone interrupted us again and probably for good measure. I was a bit surprised and needed to take a timeout before I said something stupid. I told her that I was going to get a coffee and went to the counter.

"I don't have the time," she said when I came back.

"Ok. We can talk later."

"No. I meant I don't have the time for this to take long."

"So. Then what?"

"Well, perhaps your parents can give some assurance?"

"Assurance?"

"Yes."

"Well I'm here. I am serious about you. I'm totally cool with the parents meeting."

"You know. It's going to take a while to get settled for you. You said it might be a year before it's good. So if we were to go ahead, what's going to be at our disposal if it takes a while to get settled?"

"Disposal?"

I was shocked.

"That's interesting. Where did that come from?"

"Don't misunderstand me. It's about security."

"I'm trying not to. It sounds a lot like an email I once got."

"That's just how it is Toby. This is how it's going to be."

"Interesting. And what if the assets at my disposal aren't enough?"

She shrugged and looked away.

"I only have one asset. It's my education."

"Well, think about it Toby," she said with a tone of finality.

Life is full of surprises. But the biggest ones are always those that shatter your perspective. Of all the things that I thought could go wrong, I never expected it would come down to this. Suddenly, it wasn't perfect anymore. Suddenly she was a different person.

"Why are you smiling?" she asked.

"Oh nothing. Just remembered something. Hey it's late for your flight. I have to meet a friend. Let's talk about this later."

It's funny how we randomly find small golden nuggets that seem to explain our life perfectly. I was watching The Simpsons earlier that morning. I smiled because I recalled something that Homer had told his son:

"Bart! With 100,000 dollars, we'd be millionaires! We could buy all kinds of useful things... like Love."

Toby's Journal
Entry 4, 2010

Life is many moments, many photographs tied
together.
But sometimes a rare thing happens. Sometimes a
moment lingers on... for more than a moment..

Sometimes a moment stands out, and we know in that
instant, that the story ahead is not going to be the
same; that the shades of colors will forever be
changed; and that every picture, every moment ahead
is now going to be different than what we imagined.

I had once written....

The single puddle of muddy water on the parched
broken field.
The solitary sparrow using it to shield her chicks
from the summer heat.

The bare leafless tree trying to stretch towards the
sun.
The unrelenting dew, reviving itself every morning
awaiting new green leaves.

The incessant dance of hide and seek choreographed
by the moon and the clouds.
The fleeting lonely beam of moonlight that penetrates
to illuminate the dark night.

Reality is, Hope and Despair lie in the same places.
And they're just a matter of perspective.

What changed my perspective, was her.

I was wrong.

Reality is, Hope and Despair lie in the same places.
And so does Delusion.

What changed my perspective, was her.

PART 4

11 Saudades

There is no good or evil;
or day or night.
Every right is perhaps wrong.
Every wrong is perhaps right.
(Shiv Kumar Batalvi - Often called the Punjabi Keats)

"So what happened next?" Deepak inquired.

I had come back to Chicago a couple of weeks ago and Deepak had called to hear the 'good news'. When I told him, the news wasn't good he invited himself over. We decided grab some coffee at Starbucks, as I shared my India experience with him.

"Nothing after that," I said. "I went on Sunday to the Bombay race course where Salman Khan was trying to race a bunch of professional jockeys to promote his new film. This old guy gave me a tip that if a horse shits before it races, that's considered a bad omen. I ignored him, bet on the horse and lost some money. And then flew to Chandigarh to hang out with the family."

Deepak replied sarcastically. "Oh really? It was always my dream to watch Salman Khan compete in a horse race. Tell me more!" He then added. "I meant, did you guys speak again?"

"Not really. A few times. But that was the last time we met. And then things faded. Sometimes it's not that messy. It just goes away."

"What did your parents say?"

"Well surprisingly, they weren't surprised. They said that it isn't that uncommon, especially because of the nervousness of a relationship with someone so far away. They said they could understand the emotion it came from but were surprised she was so direct about it. In fact, they even said they would be willing to sit down with her parents, if I was still interested."

"So did that make you reconsider?"

"Very fleetingly. I could understand her need for security but I just couldn't see myself with her after that. It seemed that I had been attracted to someone else. She was an entirely different person now." Maybe it was best to let things go."

'Saudades?" Deepak asked.

"What's that?"

"It's a word. Portuguese."

"Huh."

"In Arabic, it's called Wajd."

"And I know neither of those languages. Deepak, do you actually spend time preparing all these anecdotes and sifting through random words before you meet me so that you can spring them upon me?"

"Haha. No my friend, I'm just well read. I read a lot of other things when I should have been reading my engineering text books. And I read a lot of Wikipedia when I should have been working."

"Sure," I said half not believing him. "Since you've let the genie out, why don't you explain what it means?"

Deepak started his story:

"During the 15th and 16th century, the Portuguese people had a golden age where sailors traveled far and wide and mapped new lands in Africa, Asia and South America. That's when Vasco Da Gama arrived in India. However, countless other sailors never returned from their voyages."

"Ok, and this applies to me how?" I interrupted.

"Well because these sailors never came back, the people they knew were left with a mixed feeling of sadness and happiness. They were sad knowing that the person might never again be a part of their life. But they gained happiness from the fact that they did once get an opportunity to love someone. That love that remains, and the fact that there remains a slither of hope that paths might meet again is called Saudade."

"Interesting. That is a beautiful and very accurate word".

He cut me off. "In your case it's applicable twice. In the 20th century, it was also commonly used to describe the desire or longing for one's native land by thousands of Portuguese who had migrated all over the world."

"So it's the love that remains after someone or something is gone. The love that can make you happy and sad at the same time."

"Exactly!" Deepak said with a smile of content teacher on his face.

I thought for a moment. "It could be saudades then. To be honest, I was disappointed for a little bit. When you are trying to share a life with someone you are also trying to create this new world of shared hopes and expectations. That takes a lot of time and energy. I guess our worlds differed."

"Sometimes we set out on a path and realize a bit too late that where we really wanted to go was somewhere else. Luckily it was only a few months for you two," Deepak chimed.

"It felt much longer than a few months. You know in the beginning it was frustrating. I thought that it was a phenomenal waste of time. How things could have been different, better, happier if I had not met her. That it was cruel of someone up there to have dealt me this horrible set of cards. It was wrong to have let me come this close to a world that was perfect, only to take it away."

"Well that was your own illusion to build. Why blame some poor 'someone up there' for it?"

"Most of life is about building our own illusions and waiting for them to turn real or to shatter. That's how all of us would initially react, I guess. And then I saw it for what it really was."

"Which was?"

"A lesson. A discovery."

"Ahhhhh! We all have to make our own discoveries in life," he said with a cheeky smile. "I think this India trip might actually have made you a bit smarter."

"Well you always tell me stories. Let me tell you one this time around."

"Looks who's been preparing anecdotes."

I pretended to ignore him.

"During a war, an old man would come to a border checkpoint with a hand cart full of dirt. The border guard would look at his papers and everything would be in order. Yet the border guard was certain that the old man was smuggling some illegal goods in the wheelbarrow. Every single time he would search the hand cart, not find anything, and unhappily let the man past the checkpoint. Week after week, the same story repeated itself. When the war ended, the border guard asked the man. 'Old man, The war has ended. I am not a soldier now and can't do any harm to you now. One thing has bothered me and caused many sleepless nights. I knew you were smuggling something past the checkpoint. Please tell me what you were smuggling for so long?' The old man smiled and answered, 'Hand carts'"

"And your point is", Deepak asked. "You are going to start smuggling hand carts to find inner peace?"

I laughed. "The point is simple. Much in life depends on perspective and how you choose to look at the world. I could take the easy way out: sulk, complain and pass judgment. Which I initially did. Or I could try to understand her point of view and where she came from."

"My boy is learning things about the world," Deepak said. Then he changed to a serious tone. "So tell me something, do you think she was wrong?"

"I think no one was wrong here. The fact is that we wanted different things in life. Our paths crossed. We enjoyed the moments together. But in the end we couldn't find common ground to stand on. I can either look at what was lost, or look at what was gained. And what we both discovered was a deep insight into what is important for us."

"It seems she wanted stability," Deepak observed. "You were knee deep in change. I think this India trip's has definitely made you a bit smarter. So why couldn't you find common ground?"

"Fear."

"Fear of?"

"Fear of uncertainty. Fear of our differences. Fear of things not being perfect."

"How did those come?".

"Well it was beautiful when it was pure and simple. Then we became too smart for our own good. We started over analyzing everything and let our fears shape our decision."

"That created a circle of negativity," Deepak thought aloud.

"I guess all the uncertainty around the move created fears and questions. That must have started creating doubts in her mind. Gradually, those fears took a life of their own."

"And what was your fear?" he asked.

"I started to fear that it wasn't the same anymore. That she was a different person from what I thought she was. That her intentions and motivations were different from what I had thought they were."

"And that fear started sowing the seeds of doubt in your relationship."

"Right. The moment we allowed that fear to creep into our mind, we

lost sight of the beautiful world we could create together and started pondering about all the different ways things could work out badly."
"Sadly, the moment you lose that belief, you lose the drive to make things happen, the drive to find common ground," Deepak said.
"Differences are always there and they will lead to fear. What we have to realize that it's not as simple as black and white. It's shades of grey and we have the ability to change things."

My friend decided it was time for a deep thought. "Toby, someone once said: the beauty of the world is in its differences and that the beauty of humanity is that we have the power to rise beyond them. That if we can't bridge our differences, we should at the very least, be able to appreciate those differences and be comfortable with the grays in life. That we be able to make each moment count for what it's worth, without encumbering it with the past or saddling it with the future; and be able to live and enjoy many such moments and celebrate the good we find."
"Yes. If we'd understood that, things could have been different. She was right from her perspective. I was right where I was. We couldn't bridge our differences and find common ground to stand on." I paused and then asked sheepishly, "If you knew all that, why couldn't you share it before?"

"We all have to discover the secrets of life in our own ways. You know, Shiv Kumar Batalvi said it best."
"Shiv who?" I had never heard that name before.
"He was a great Punjabi poet. He said:

'*There is no good or evil; or day or night.*
Every right is perhaps wrong. Every wrong is perhaps right.'"

"That sounds good. I will use that in my book."
"Make sure I am in there. My Nadi leaf said I'll be a famous philosopher."
"As long as you buy a copy."
"Deal."

We shook hands.

"What about your other saudade?" Deepak asked.
"The other saudade?" I asked slowly, wondering if I had missed something.
"The desire to go back home."
"Haha. I don't know. Maybe it's time to go back home. Maybe it's too late now. Let's see how the dice rolls."
"Déjà vu. Only someone else who's moved far away from home can understand the dichotomy of staying where you are and the longing to go back home."

Then he stopped laughing, leaned in and put on a serious expression.
"So, tell me something important"
"What?" I asked.
He smiled. "When was the last time you had a beer?"
"Haha. You're so predictable. Let's go."

As we walked into the bar, Deepak put his hand on my shoulder.
"So my girlfriend has this friend who's got bad enough judgment to be slightly interested in you."
"Must have really bad judgment then."
"She's sweet, good looking, moved here for her Masters and works near your office, and.."
"And…"
"And best of all."
"Best of all?" This can't be good, I thought to myself.
"I'm going to make my girlfriend mention to her that your ass is broke as hell and I'm pretty sure she wouldn't care."
"Ass."

RICHIE SINGH

12 Epiphanies

(well you can't really end a book with 'ass')

Toby's Journal
Entry 13, 2010

Perhaps the greatest joy of childhood is how spartan and innocent it is.

Yes. No.
Like. Not like.
Want. Do not want.

The words we know are limited, as is our knowledge of the world.

Then we are taught new words, we learn new things and are told to start analyzing for alternatives.

Maybe. More.

Irony is:

the more words we learn, the less we communicate,
the more things we know, the less we understand,
the more alternatives we create, the less happy we get.

As a child we were all brimming with hope. We could appreciate what we had and yet celebrate our differences. We could enjoy the moment yet dream about a beautiful tomorrow:

A legendary love story.
A storybook castle.
A frog that turns into a prince, or
A beautiful princess waiting on a high tower.

Then we were given fears:

Fear of uncertainty.
Fear of losing.
Fear of being different.
Fear of not being perfect

We were told of a new reality. A world where:

Legendary love stories are almost always tragic.
Storybook castles can foreclose.
Frogs have a tendency to stay frogs no matter how much you may make out with them.
And behind the princess on the high tower is a witch's curse and a fire breathing dragon.

Somewhere in that sea of fear and doubt and the quest for perfection, we lost our humanity. After all, only fools chase thin air wishing a butterfly would materialize out of it, or fall in love with a flower that will fade away.

After all, in this cruel world:

It doesn't make sense to chase thin air.
It doesn't make sense to admire something that will go away.

It doesn't make sense to fall in love with someone or something you don't fully understand or predict.

So why chase thin air or pluck a flower that will fade?

Because:

Sometimes we end up keeping the flower in a book only to admire its beauty years later.
Sometimes we have to believe that a butterfly might materialize out of thin air.
Sometimes we have to let go of our fears, and allow the butterfly to come to us.
Sometimes it's not even about the butterfly at the end, but what the chase brought us.

Sometimes we have to take a deep breath, appreciate that things aren't perfect and it takes effort to overcome our fears, and that is where lies the true beauty of this world!

Sometimes we have to take a leap of faith, and choose to be human, in a world that's not.

RICHIE SINGH

ABOUT THE AUTHOR

Richie Singh lives in Santa Monica, California and likes chasing butterflies. Having moved to the US for further studies in 1999, he writes as a hobby and likes to explore stories centered around the uniqueness of the immigrant experience. This is his first novel.

And if you are wondering whether Toby did find love or moved back; the journey of Toby Arora will continue with the second novel out in late 2012

Connect with Richie at stay apprised of upcoming work, exclusive content and free giveaways of autographed copies at www.chasingbutterflies.me

Cheers!